FROM THE
NANCY DREW FILES

THE CASE: A deadly threat to rock star Adam Sledge puts Nancy on alert and in major danger.

CONTACT: Frank Cassone, the chef at Reverb, invites Nancy, Bess, and George to opening night at the restaurant.

SUSPECTS: Whitney Washington—*Sledge's former girlfriend owns a rival restaurant, giving her two good reasons to take him down.*

Frank Cassone—*Sledge repeatedly threatens to fire the chef, who may have cooked up a bit of a surprise for his boss.*

Larry Sen—*Sledge's manager wants the rock star to pay more attention to his music and wouldn't mind seeing Reverb go up in smoke.*

COMPLICATION: Sparks are flying between Nancy and Adam Sledge, and if any of them hit home, her relationship with Ned could end up getting burned!

Books in The Nancy Drew Files® Series

Available from ARCHWAY Paperbacks

The Nancy Drew Files™
117

SKIPPING A BEAT

CAROLYN KEENE

AN ARCHWAY PAPERBACK
Published by POCKET BOOKS
New York London Toronto Sydney Tokyo Singapore

This book is a work of fiction. Names, characters, places and incidents are products of the author's imagination or are used fictitiously. Any resemblance to actual events or locales or persons, living or dead, is entirely coincidental.

AN ARCHWAY PAPERBACK *Original*

An Archway Paperback published by
POCKET BOOKS, a division of Simon & Schuster Inc.
1230 Avenue of the Americas, New York, NY 10020

ISBN: 0-671-56875-2

First Archway Paperback printing October 1996

10 9 8 7 6 5 4 3 2

Printed in the U.S.A.

IL 6+

SKIPPING A BEAT

Chapter

One

Y OU LOOK GORGEOUS in that black dress, Nan!"
Bess Marvin said to Nancy Drew.

Nancy's blue eyes sparkled. "Thanks. You look
great, too. That dress you bought today fits you
perfectly."

George Fayne, who wasn't very interested in
clothes, groaned impatiently. "All of the guys in
Chicago are going to flip over you two. But first
they have to *see* you. And that means we have to
get out the door!"

Nancy and her two best friends were in Chicago for a few days' vacation. They'd already
enjoyed plenty of shopping and museum hop-
ping. Now they were dressed and ready for the
highlight of the trip, the opening of Reverb, a hot
new theme restaurant. The restaurant was owned
by Adam Sledge, the lead singer and guitarist for

1

Void, a rock band whose last three albums had hit the top of the charts.

Even though George was pretending to be annoyed, Nancy knew she, too, had put a lot of thought into what she would wear that evening. George's dress was simple and classic, and Nancy thought that red looked great with George's dark hair. And George looked even prettier than usual because her dark eyes were glowing with excitement. She'd been anticipating this evening for weeks.

George was looking forward to getting reacquainted with Frank Cassone, a young chef at Reverb. Frank had grown up in River Heights, and his parents were friendly with George's parents. When he'd learned from his mother that George, Bess, and Nancy were going to be in town, he'd offered to put them on the guest list for the restaurant's opening night. George was thrilled because, even though Frank was some years older than she, she'd always had a crush on him.

Bess took one last look in the mirror. "I'm ready," she announced decisively.

Nancy picked up her shoulder bag, her coat, and her car keys. "Then let's go."

"Just think," Bess said as the girls stepped out into the hotel corridor, "in a few minutes, we could be meeting Adam Sledge."

George laughed lightly as she closed the door to their room. "If I know you, Bess, you'll have a date with every member of Void before the night is over."

Bess and George were cousins, but they couldn't have been more different. George was a top athlete who could sometimes be shy about guys. Bess was a major flirt who seemed to fall in and out of love on an average of once a week.

Nancy walked down the hallway in front of the others and pushed the button for the elevator. When it arrived, the girls stepped inside and rode down to the underground parking garage. They quickly climbed into Nancy's blue Mustang.

Nancy pulled out of the garage into traffic. The tall, brightly lit buildings towered above them. It was a warm fall evening, and groups of people were strolling down the street, window shopping and checking out the restaurants.

Bess sighed happily as she looked out the car window. "I love this city! It's so exciting."

"It's also confusing," Nancy said as she passed Bess a street map of Chicago. "Tell me where to turn."

"Bess Marvin, glamour navigator, reporting for duty," Bess said.

Fifteen minutes later the girls parked the car in the restaurant parking lot and were walking toward Reverb. "Check out this scene!" Bess exclaimed. Throngs of people had gathered around the front of the restaurant. "It's wild!"

"I hope all these people aren't here for the private party," George said.

"I'm sure they're here to see Adam Sledge," Bess said.

Nancy took a closer look at the crowd and decided Bess was right. A lot of the people were wearing black Void concert T-shirts. But Nancy also noticed several people who were carrying tape recorders or cameras with huge zoom lenses. They had to be reporters and professional photographers, Nancy thought. And although she didn't see any camera crews, she noted several local television vans parked in front of the restaurant.

"Look over there." Bess pointed to a group of girls who were standing together and chanting Adam's name. "That must be one of Adam's fan clubs."

Nancy's eyes were sparkling with amusement. "If you don't get a date with Adam tonight, maybe you can join."

"I'll consider it," Bess said. "Hey, what's with all that light?" Reverb's main entrance was flooded with bright light.

Nancy looked behind her and saw a huge spotlight mounted on a truck. She nodded her head in the direction of the truck. "It's a spotlight. Reverb probably rented it for the evening."

George laughed as the girls fought their way up to the door. "I feel like I'm at the Oscars."

"Good evening," a burly man in a tuxedo greeted them. "May I help you?"

"We're on the guest list," George told him. "The name is Fayne."

The man studied a long list attached to a black plastic clipboard.

Bess grabbed Nancy's arm. "Whitney Washington is here! That must be who the TV reporters are interviewing!"

Nancy stood on her tiptoes, trying to see around the lights and cameramen. She caught only a glimpse of a tall, stunning woman with smooth, chocolate-colored skin and a hip, layered haircut, but she immediately recognized her. Whitney Washington had starred in a movie Nancy had seen a few months earlier with her boyfriend, Ned Nickerson. The movie had been pretty awful, but Nancy and Ned had both agreed that Whitney looked terrific.

"She's even prettier in person," Nancy told Bess.

"*Pretty* celebrities don't interest me much," Bess replied. "I'm more into the handsome type. But maybe I'll have better luck inside."

Nancy laughed. "Knowing you, Bess, I'm *sure* you will."

"Fayne. Three," the security guard said. "Okay, you can go in."

As Nancy, George, and Bess stepped forward, a strobe went off in their faces.

"Thank you!" a dark-haired man with a press pass around his neck said as he lowered his camera. "By the way, who are you?"

"Sorry, nobody famous," Nancy replied quickly.

"At least, not yet," Bess said, tossing her blond hair over her shoulder.

"Whew!" Nancy said as the girls stepped inside. "That was quite a scene."

"Only about half as big as the one in here," Bess said enthusiastically.

The restaurant was pulsating with voices and loud music. The room itself was dimly lit, but small spotlights shone on each table. Most of the tables were full, and groups of people crowded around the gleaming ebony bar and elaborate buffet. This crowd, however, was nothing like the one outside. A number of the men were wearing tuxedos, and many of the women looked as if they had stepped straight from the pages of a fashion magazine. "Talk about glamorous," George said to Nancy. "I'm glad you convinced me to wear a dress."

"I think I see an empty table back there," Bess said, pointing toward the rear of the room. "Let's grab it and then we can go check out the food."

"I'm more interested in checking out the crowd," George said. "Look, there's Lili Taylor!"

"Really? Where?" Bess gasped. Lili Taylor played a deranged nurse on Bess's favorite soap opera. "Oh, I see her! Wow, what a dress. It's so tiny!"

"Should we go say hi to her?" Nancy asked.

"I don't think so," Bess said. "She has a habit of poisoning people."

George laughed. "Not to mention stabbing them with needles."

Nancy kept an eye out for celebrities as she followed her friends to the table. She was almost certain she recognized Clay Parker, a muscle-bound movie star who had played the hero in countless action movies. Nancy was dazzled. Being at a party with so many celebrities was really fun.

By some miracle, the table Bess had seen from the door was still empty when Nancy and the others got to it. They put down their coats on the chairs to save the table and then doubled back to the buffet.

"Yummy!" Although Bess always claimed to be on a diet, she didn't let that stop her from enjoying good food whenever the opportunity arose. And the buffet before them was enough to tempt even the most determined weight watcher.

"Do you think Frank made all this?" Nancy asked as she helped herself to some grilled chicken salad.

"Probably not all of it," George said, reaching for some jumbo shrimp. "He told me that Reverb has two chefs. Frank is in charge of brunch and lunch. There's another chef at dinner."

After the girls filled their plates, they headed back to the table. But before she sat down, Nancy stopped to admire a brilliant red electric guitar that was hanging on the wall above a small brass plaque. "That guitar belonged to Jimi Hendrix," Nancy told her friends as she slid into her seat.

"Really?" George's eyes widened.

"Really," came a deep voice. A tall, slender

young man with wavy black hair and olive skin was standing over their table. He was wearing a chef's jacket and holding a dessert plate.

"Frank!" George exclaimed. "How are you?"

"Great," Frank said. "Having fun?"

"Definitely," George said. "Thanks so much for getting us in. I think we're the only people here who aren't famous."

"I'm glad you could come," Frank said.

Bess leaned forward to examine the dessert plate that Frank placed on the table. On it was a chocolate dessert in the shape of a guitar, with white icing for the strings.

"That's incredible!" Bess told Frank.

"Did you make it?" Nancy asked.

"Actually, no," Frank admitted. "That's the work of our pastry chef, Meghan. I brought it out because I remembered how much George loves chocolate."

Nancy noticed George's pleased smile. Frank wasn't wasting much time. They'd barely said hello and he was already flirting.

"It looks too fabulous to eat," Nancy commented.

"It tastes even better than it looks," Frank said. "Everything Meghan makes is delicious, but this is her masterpiece."

"Don't worry," Bess said wryly. "I couldn't resist even if I wanted to."

"So, how has your stay in Chicago been so far?" Frank asked.

Nancy and Bess listened while George answered Frank's questions about their weekend. The two immediately became so wrapped up in each other, they seemed to forget that Bess and Nancy were there.

Nancy gave Bess a wink, which she returned. Both girls were pleased to see that Frank was just as attracted to George as she was to him.

"Oh—here comes Whitney Washington!" Bess exclaimed, pointing toward the door.

Frank's eyebrows shot up. He discreetly turned and looked over his shoulder, then turned back to the girls. "You're right," he said. "I can't believe it."

"Why not?" Nancy commented. "This place is filled with celebrities."

"Yes, but Whitney isn't just a celebrity. She's also Adam's ex-girlfriend," Frank told them. "Not to mention the fact that she owns a restaurant—which she named after herself—a few blocks away. I can't believe she'd want to help Adam hype this place."

"Maybe she came to check out the competition," George suggested.

"Or maybe she just didn't want to miss a great party," Nancy said with a laugh.

"See the man who just walked up to her?" Frank whispered.

Nancy sat up straighter so that she could see the scene unfolding near the door. A balding man with a neatly trimmed reddish beard, wearing an expensive Italian suit, was giving the elegant actress a kiss on the cheek. She looked bored.

"Who is he?" Nancy asked.

"Adam's agent," Frank said in a confidential tone. "He's a major player in Hollywood. He represents most of the big names in rock. His name is Larry Sen, but the restaurant staff calls him Mr. Network. I'd place a bet that he doesn't sit down this whole evening. He's got working a crowd down to a science."

"Do you recognize any other—" Bess broke off as a tall woman dressed in an exquisite emerald-colored dress approached the table.

"Oh, great," Frank mumbled under his breath. "Here comes trouble."

"I've been looking all over for you," the woman greeted Frank. "Adam wants to talk to you immediately."

Frank gave the woman an impish smile. "Hi, Paula," he said. "These are my friends from River Heights."

"Pleased to meet you," Paula said. She gave the girls a forced smile and then turned her attention back to Frank. "Adam's in the kitchen. Don't keep him waiting." With that, Paula moved off into the crowd.

Frank turned toward the girls with an apologetic smile.

"Did we get you in trouble somehow?" George asked.

Frank shook his head, looking more amused than angry. "Nah, Paula always acts that way. She's the day-to-day manager of this place. She's here like twenty-three hours a day, so she's usually pretty stressed out."

"The Adam who's waiting to see you—is that Adam Sledge?" Bess asked shyly.

Frank rolled his eyes. "That's the one. Mr. God's-gift-to-rock-and-women himself."

"You don't sound as if you like Adam much," Nancy commented.

"Well, Adam makes Paula seem calm by comparison," Frank said with an exasperated laugh. "He threatens to fire me about six times a day."

The girls exchanged surprised looks. So far, working for a rock star didn't seem like a whole lot of fun.

"Does Adam actually work here?" Nancy asked Frank. "I thought most celebrities who are involved with places like this just put up the money and then jet back to L.A."

"That's true," Frank said. "But Adam is a real hands-on kind of guy. He's willing to work hard to make it a success. But if it's popular, he'll really clean up."

"Smart guy," Bess said.

"He's not stupid," Frank admitted. "But I think Whitney gave him the idea. She keeps close tabs on her place, too. Rumor has it that she made a cool million last year just from the T-shirts and other merchandise she sells."

11

"Wow!" George said.

"Pretty unbelievable, huh?" Frank said, shaking his head. "Well, I probably should go see what Adam wants. He gets irritated if you keep him waiting. But I'll come back out and see how you all are doing in about an hour. I want to know how you like the food!"

"Later, then," George said.

"'Bye," Nancy and Bess said together.

Frank gave them all a little wave and then disappeared into the crowd.

"I think I know why Frank invited us tonight," Nancy said as she finally picked up her fork.

"Me, too," Bess put in.

"What are you guys talking about?" George demanded. "Frank just did it to be nice."

"Come off it," Bess said. "Frank is obviously trying to impress you."

"Do you think so?" George asked with a hopeful grin.

"Absolutely," Nancy said.

"He's gotten even more handsome since he left River Heights, don't you think?" George asked.

"Absolutely," Bess said with a giggle.

George sighed happily. "Nothing could ruin this evening," she said.

Nancy smiled, happy to see her friend feeling so good. But a moment later her smile faded. Nancy smelled a familiar odor. Although it was extremely faint, it was enough to make her sit up straight.

"Do you smell smoke?" Nancy asked, looking

around and noticing for the first time just how dangerously crowded the restaurant had become.

George's seat faced out into the restaurant. "I smell it and I see it!" she exclaimed.

Nancy quickly spun around just in time to see clouds of dense, dark smoke engulfing the restaurant!

Chapter

Two

NANCY YANKED the cloth napkins off the table and dunked them in her water glass as the thick smoke rapidly filled the restaurant. "Cover your mouths with these," she told Bess and George, who were already beginning to cough a little. The napkins would keep them from inhaling the worst of the smoke.

Nancy looked warily at the crowd. Only moments before, the room had felt festive, filled with laughter and music. But now the mood was threatening. Nancy knew that few things were more dangerous than a panicked mob. And this crowd was definitely starting to panic.

"I can't breathe!" a tall man near the kitchen gasped as he began to push through the crowd. "I have to get out of here!"

A woman at the next table was gripping the

14

armrests of her chair so hard that her knuckles were white. "I think it's time to go," her date said in a frightened tone. But the woman, like a deer caught in someone's headlights, seemed unable to move. "Fire," she whispered, her eyes round with fear.

Bess scrambled to her feet just as a man pushing past her knocked her chair over.

"Where *is* the fire?" Nancy stood tall to get a better view of the room.

"I don't see any flames," Bess panted. "Just smoke."

George, who was the tallest of the three, stretched up on her tiptoes and looked around. "The door won't open," she reported, her voice muffled by the damp napkin.

"Why not?" Nancy demanded. "Is it locked?"

George shook her head. "I think it's because the door swings in," she explained. "But so many people are pushing against it there's no room to open it." George paused and fought to catch her breath. "The people near the door can't step back. Too many people are pushing against them."

A high-pitched shriek came from the crowd.

Bess's eyes widened in alarm. "What happened?"

"Someone slipped," George reported. "She's trying to get up, but the crowd won't give her room. She's going to get trampled!"

Nancy stepped out of her high-heeled shoes and quickly climbed up onto the girls' table. She put two fingers between her lips and let out a shrill whistle. Instantly the room grew considerably quieter.

"Listen up!" Nancy yelled in a calm, commanding voice. "Everyone, listen to me now!"

Through the smoke, Nancy could see that the crowd was slowly turning toward her. They seemed drawn to her take-charge attitude. Nancy knew she didn't have long to act. Smoke rises, and as she stood on the table, waiting for the crowd to quiet down, Nancy felt as if her lungs were being poisoned by the dense, acrid air. She forced herself to ignore the choking feeling in her lungs and the tears burning her eyes. But she wasn't sure how long she could hold out.

"Don't panic!" Nancy said as soon as she had everyone's attention. "Everything is fine. But if we want to get out of here, we're going to have to calm down and work together."

While Nancy was talking, George made her way toward the injured woman, who was now sitting on the floor, holding her ankle and sobbing.

"We need room to open the door," Nancy said. "So, I want everyone on the steps to move back toward the center of the room."

Nobody moved. "Come on, people, put it in gear!" Nancy barked.

She was relieved when the crowd slowly began to inch away from the door. A tuxedo-clad man stepped forward and swung the door open. The crowd instantly surged forward.

George helped the injured woman to her feet. The woman leaned against George and hopped toward the door.

Bess held out a hand and helped Nancy off the table. "Let's get out of here," she gasped, picking up their coats and bags. "This smoke is really starting to get to me."

By then the crowd ahead of them had cleared the room. Some of the smoke had been drawn out of the open door, but it was still thick enough to send Bess into a coughing fit as she and Nancy hurried outside.

"Fresh air!" Bess paused on the doorstep to take her first deep breath. "Delicious!"

Nancy caught her breath, then bent over to put her heels back on. As she was shrugging on her coat she heard sirens.

The crowd was huddling in groups outside the restaurant. They were talking quietly and casting fearful glances at the building, as if expecting it to burst into flames.

The same reporters who had been interviewing celebrities earlier in the evening were now rushing around pressing people for details of what had happened inside. Nancy noticed one teary woman point her out to a reporter.

"Look, there's Adam," Bess said.

Nancy looked toward where Bess was pointing. But all she could see was a crowd of newspeople.

"We're definitely not going to meet him now," Nancy said as the fire trucks, an ambulance, and at least half a dozen police cruisers came screeching to a stop in front of the restaurant, sirens blaring.

The firefighters jumped out of their trucks and rushed toward the building. The police weren't far behind, encircling the crowd and gently moving them away from the building.

"There's George," Bess said, pointing toward the street.

A middle-aged man was helping George carry the injured woman toward the ambulance. Bess and Nancy made their way through the crowd, carefully ducking the TV news crews and reporters. By the time they reached the ambulance, the hurt woman was in the hands of the paramedics.

"How is she?" Nancy called as she and Bess approached George.

"Fine, I think," George reported. "She may have sprained her ankle. But I don't think she broke it or anything. How are you guys?"

"Fine," Nancy said.

"Glad to be out of that crowd," Bess added with a shudder.

"Me, too," George said.

"George! Nancy! Bess!"

The girls turned and saw Frank waving at them. He was standing with a group of people a few yards down the sidewalk.

"Come on," George said, starting toward him. Nancy and Bess followed.

"I'm so glad you're all okay." Frank was visibly relieved as he greeted the girls.

"Same here," George told him. "How did you and the rest of the staff get out? We didn't see you."

"Paula hustled us out the back door as soon as she saw the smoke," Frank explained. "We didn't open the door to the dining room because we were afraid the fire might spread into the kitchen."

Nancy gave Frank a curious look. "You were afraid of spreading the fire *into* the kitchen?" she repeated. "Isn't that where the fire started?"

Frank shook his head. "There wasn't a fire in the kitchen."

"That's weird," Bess said. "I saw a lot of smoke, but I didn't actually see anything on fire in the dining room, either."

"It could have been an electrical fire," George said. "I think those can start in the walls."

Nancy was fairly certain a fire started by faulty wiring wouldn't have produced so much smoke so quickly. But she kept her opinion to herself. She gave her friends a reassuring smile and nodded toward the fire trucks. "Well, I'm sure we'll find out soon."

"Hey, Frank, did you find out what's going on?" A woman in her early twenties wearing chef's whites peeked around Frank's shoulder. "Oh, I'm sorry, am I interrupting?"

"No, it's cool," Frank said. "Meghan, I want you to meet some of my friends from home. This is George, Nancy, and Bess."

"Hi," Meghan said shyly. "Were you guys inside?"

"Yeah," Bess said. "I've never seen a party break up so quickly. Hey, you aren't the pastry chef, by any chance, are you?"

Meghan shot Frank a questioning look. "Yes, that's me," she admitted.

"Frank brought one of your beautiful desserts out to us," Bess said. "I was just getting ready to eat it when the dining room started filling up with smoke."

Meghan smiled at Bess's praise. "You'll have to come by the restaurant again. There's more where that came from."

As Meghan and Bess talked, Nancy noticed that George and Frank had fallen into an intense conversation, and even in the unsettling atmosphere, seemed to be having a great time. Nancy turned her attention back to what Bess and Meghan were discussing.

"So what's it like working for Adam Sledge?" Bess asked in an envious voice. "Working for a rock star, I mean."

"It was a thrill at first," Meghan admitted. "But now he pretty much seems like any boss—loud and obnoxious. Sort of like his music."

"Don't you like Void?" Nancy asked Meghan.

Meghan shrugged. "They're okay, I guess," she said, running both hands through her streaky blond hair. "Do you?"

Before Nancy could answer, George walked

over and said, "It looks like the firefighters are coming out now." George pointed to them.

"Great," Nancy said. "Let's ask them what they found inside." The girls said goodbye to Meghan and Frank, then quickly made their way toward the firefighters. But the firefighters were immediately surrounded by reporters. Nancy, George, and Bess stood behind the newspeople, straining to hear what the spokesman for the firefighters was saying.

Whatever it was didn't hold the reporters' attention for long. The group started to break up after just a couple of minutes.

"What did they say?" Nancy asked a young woman who was holding a microphone on a boom.

The woman looked a bit disappointed. "No fire," she reported. "They said all they found were a couple of smoke bombs. One near the kitchen and one in the main dining area. Nothing but a harmless prank."

"Thanks," Nancy said.

The woman shrugged. "You can hear all about it on the late news. Channel six."

George shook her head as the woman walked away. "I wouldn't exactly call this a harmless prank," she commented.

"I wouldn't either," Nancy agreed. "We practically had a riot inside."

"Not to mention that Reverb's opening is ruined," Bess added. "This is going to cost Adam Sledge big bucks. And we're out a free dinner."

"What should we do now?" George asked the others as she watched people drift toward the parking lot or get into waiting limousines and taxicabs.

"I don't know," Nancy admitted. "But this party is definitely over." She was disappointed that their big night in Chicago had been ruined.

"Listen, I'm starving," Bess told the others. "Let's go grab a pizza."

"Sounds good to me," Nancy said. "But I think we should go to the fanciest pizza joint we can find. After all, we're not exactly dressed down."

"We might look good," George commented. "But we smell like a barbecue."

Nancy made a face. "You're right. Forget fancy. We'll be lucky if any place lets us in."

The girls were laughing as they started toward Nancy's car.

"Well, at least the evening wasn't a complete waste," Bess commented. "We did manage to see Frank. Are you going to see him again before we go home?" she asked George.

"Definitely," George said, a faraway smile on her face. "He said he'd call tomorrow and—"

"Shh!" Bess hissed. "Here he comes."

"George! Nancy!" Frank called. "Wait! Don't go!"

The girls turned and watched Frank run toward them. As he got closer, Nancy realized that something was wrong. Frank's confident manner from earlier in the evening was completely gone. He looked desperate, even scared.

"I'm glad you're still here," he gasped once he caught up with them. He put his hands on his knees and leaned over to catch his breath.

George put her hand on Frank's back. "Is everything okay?" she asked with concern.

"No," Frank gasped. "You have to come back to the restaurant right away!"

Chapter

Three

"WHY?" NANCY ASKED. "What's happening?"

Frank had recovered enough from his mad dash to give the girls a weak smile. "Adam Sledge wants to meet you, Nancy," he explained. "I'm afraid that if I hadn't found you, I would've been fired for real."

"Adam Sledge wants to meet *me?*" Nancy asked in surprise.

"He doesn't *want* to meet you," Frank replied. "He's *demanding* to meet you."

"That's so cool!" George said with excitement.

"Can we come, too?" Bess asked eagerly.

"Sure," Frank told her. "Adam is used to people who travel with an entourage. You and George can be Nancy's."

"But why would Adam demand to see me?"

Nancy persisted. "How does Adam even know my name?"

"Because I told him all about you," Frank said.

Nancy was beginning to catch on. "All about me?"

Frank nodded. "Especially about your amazing crime-solving ability. Adam's pretty broken up about what happened here tonight. I knew you'd want to help."

"Well, I'm not promising I'll get involved," Nancy told him. "But I *am* willing to meet Adam and hear what he has to say. At the very least, it'll be a good story to tell Ned."

"Terrific," Frank said. "Follow me. I'll take you to his office."

"I don't believe this is happening!" Bess said as the girls hurried after Frank. "I'm really going to meet Adam Sledge tonight! Do I look okay?"

"You look great," Nancy reassured her friend. Normally she would have teased Bess about getting so excited. But the truth was, Nancy felt a bit giddy herself. After all, it's wasn't every day that she got to meet a major rock star!

Frank led the girls into the restaurant through the kitchen door. Meghan and several other members of the kitchen staff were clearing away the food they had been preparing earlier. They stopped working and watched as Frank led the girls through the kitchen, but Frank didn't offer the staff any explanation.

Nancy noted that the smoke bomb didn't seem to have harmed the kitchen. Adam should be glad there wasn't a real fire here tonight, she thought.

Frank approached a door bearing a brass sign that read The Boss. He rapped firmly on the door.

"Come in!" called a voice from inside.

Frank opened the door and motioned for the girls to enter before him. Bess, Nancy, George, and Frank stepped inside.

Adam Sledge was leaning back in a luxurious leather chair, his feet up on an enormous mahogany desk. Nancy couldn't help noticing his obviously expensive black-and-white snakeskin cowboy boots.

Paula was sitting in a plastic straight-backed chair in front of the desk. Even after all the commotion, her dress was spotless, and her shoulder-length hair held its perfect pageboy style. Only Paula's posture—she was holding her back rigid as she leaned toward Adam— indicated to Nancy how much stress she was under.

Nancy's heart skipped a beat as Adam removed his feet from the desk and stood up to greet her. She had several Void CDs in her collection at home, and she had seen numerous photographs of Adam in magazines, but she had never noticed exactly how handsome the band's lead singer and guitarist was. Now, seeing him up close, she realized that Adam contributed more than his considerable musical talent to the band's enormous popularity. He was more than handsome, he was mesmerizing. His glossy black hair reached halfway down his back, and he was wearing a diamond stud in one ear. His intelligent-looking green eyes swept over Nancy, and he smiled, as if he liked what he saw.

"Adam, this is Nancy Drew," Frank said.

Adam raised one eyebrow as Nancy held out her hand. "So you're Frank's detective friend?" he said. "I was expecting a tough-looking, overweight woman in a trench coat."

"Sorry to disappoint you," Nancy replied, smiling.

"Oh, I'm not disappointed," Adam said, and grinned.

Nancy felt herself blushing and hoped it didn't show.

"These are my friends," she said quickly. "Bess Marvin and George Fayne."

"I'm a big fan," Bess said enthusiastically. "Thanks so much for letting us come tonight."

"Adam," Paula snapped, "we have a major problem on our hands here. Is this really a good time for a visit from your fan club?"

"Now, now, Paula," Adam said as he gracefully lowered himself back into his chair. "Play nice. Frank says that back where he comes from, Nancy is considered an all-star detective."

"Yes, and Frank comes from River Heights," Paula said, dismissing them with a wave of her hand. "We don't need some small-town teenager helping us. I'm quite sure I can handle this on my own."

"What makes you think that?" Adam demanded. "As I recall, your résumé didn't mention any stints as a private eye."

"Of course it didn't!" Paula replied hotly. "But nobody knows more about running a restaurant than I do. And I can promise you that having this little, er, Nancy and her friends poking around here will make running this place practically impossible."

Boy, she's really overreacting, Nancy thought. I wonder why she's so bothered by us? Is it possible she's hiding something?

Adam caught Nancy's eye. He seemed to be waiting to see what she had to say. Nancy held Adam's gaze, but she didn't say anything. She made a point of never working for anyone unless that person had full confidence in her. So even though she was curious about who had planted the smoke bombs, she remained silent and let Adam make up his own mind about what to do next.

"Did you hear me, Adam?" Paula demanded. "I don't want this girl poking around while I'm trying to get this restaurant going."

"Sorry, Paula," Adam said, without taking his eyes off Nancy. "But I think having Nancy around will be cool. Besides, she's cute."

Nancy felt a little zap inside. Adam Sledge was flirting with her!

"You're hired," Adam told Nancy. "Now, let's

get down to business. Everyone have a seat, please."

Nancy sat down in the chair Frank offered her. She could hear George and Bess getting settled behind her.

"This shouldn't be a tough case even for a small-town detective," Adam told Nancy confidently. "I know who's guilty."

Nancy raised her eyebrows in surprise. "You do?"

"Sure," Adam said with a shrug. "Whitney Washington."

"Why would Whitney want to ruin your opening night?" Nancy asked.

"Because I dumped her," Adam said matter-of-factly. "She was devastated. And getting revenge is just her style."

"Do you really think she's capable of setting smoke bombs?" Nancy asked. "Someone could have been hurt."

Adam laughed harshly. "Capable? She'd love it. Listen, you don't get to the top of the modeling business without playing rough. And, as I'm sure you know, Whitney got to the very top before she became an actress."

"Besides, it's obvious Whitney has another motive," Paula offered.

"Yes, I know," Nancy said crisply. "She owns a restaurant nearby."

"How did you know that?" Paula sounded surprised.

"I may be a small-town detective, but I'm not

completely clueless," Nancy told Paula with a smile aimed at Adam. "It makes sense that Whitney wouldn't be thrilled with the competition from Reverb."

Adam snorted. "She's *definitely* not pleased."

"Revenge and greed," Nancy mused. "Those are two good motives. I'll talk to Whitney."

"Good," Adam said. "Well, keep in touch." With that, Adam picked up the receiver of the phone and punched in a number. Apparently, the meeting was over.

"One more thing," Nancy said as she got to her feet.

Adam raised his eyebrows, as if surprised anyone would have anything more to say. He slowly hung up the phone. "Yes?"

"Whoever did this may try something else," Nancy said. "Do you have any security at the restaurant?"

"We have two security guards who work out front," Paula told her. "But their job is to keep the crowd orderly. They're only on duty when the restaurant is open."

"That's probably fine for now," Nancy said. "Would you ask them to stay alert for anything out of the ordinary?"

Paula looked annoyed, but she nodded.

"You may also be in danger," Nancy told Adam. "Do you have a bodyguard?"

Adam shook his head impatiently. "I don't need a bodyguard. I fight my own fights."

"Still, sometimes it's nice to have someone

watching your back," Nancy said mildly. "If you like, I could ask around and get a recommendation."

"No bodyguards," Adam said firmly.

"But—" Nancy started.

Adam picked up the phone and hit the redial button. It was clear they had reached the end of the discussion.

Frank stepped forward. "Come on, you guys. I'll walk you to your car," he said.

"Thanks," Nancy said.

"So, what did you think of Adam?" Frank asked once they were outside.

"He's a bit full of himself," George commented.

"Totally," Bess agreed.

Nancy glanced at her friends in surprise. "That's a bit harsh. I just thought that he had a strong personality. And he's obviously used to being in charge."

"He hardly acknowledged our existence," Bess said, sounding a little hurt.

"And did anyone notice the way he assumed Whitney was devastated when he broke up with her?" George said.

"We don't know that he was assuming that," Nancy argued. "Maybe Whitney told him that was how she felt."

"Uh-oh," Frank said in an amused voice. "Adam's charm strikes again. Nancy, I do believe you find your latest client attractive."

Nancy felt her face redden. But when she

31

considered it, she realized Frank was probably right. Don't get carried away, she told herself. Anyway, it was silly to even consider an attraction to Adam. He was a major rock star, who could probably date any girl he wanted; she wasn't egotistical enough to assume he would pick her.

"I guess it's fair to say I didn't find Adam as obnoxious as Bess and George did," Nancy told Frank. "You have to expect someone so rich and so famous to be a little arrogant, don't you think?"

"Maybe," Frank allowed. "But it seems like that particular kind of arrogance doesn't bother you."

Nancy gave Frank a wink. "I think I can handle it."

The group had reached Nancy's car.

"Well, I'll say goodbye to you here," Frank said. "Adam plans to open the restaurant for brunch tomorrow, and I have to make sure everything is ready. But I'll see you all again, right?"

"Of course!" George exclaimed.

"We'll stop by the restaurant tomorrow," Nancy said. "I want to ask the other employees some questions."

"Great," Frank said.

"See you then," George said.

Nancy unlocked her car and the girls got in. Frank gave them one last wave and then headed back toward the restaurant.

"Frank's really in no position to tease me about crushes," Nancy said with feigned indignance as she started the car.

"What do you mean?" George asked innocently.

"Oh, please!" Bess said to George as Nancy started the car. "The sparks were really flying between you and Frank. Maybe that's why there were so many fire engines at the restaurant tonight," she added with a laugh.

George sighed happily. "Oh, that."

"So, can we go and get something to eat now?" Bess asked as Nancy pulled into traffic.

"Excellent idea," Nancy said. "And I have just the place. I think we should go over to Whitney's restaurant. Maybe she'll be there, and we can check out our number one suspect."

"Sounds good to me," George said.

"We can check her out and eat, too," Bess commented from the backseat. "I'm starving."

"That can be our cover," Nancy said with a grin. "We'll go into the restaurant posing as hungry people." She looked in her rearview mirror at Bess. "Bess, did you happen to bring your guidebook with you tonight? I need to know where Whitney's place is located."

Bess opened her shoulder bag and pulled out her guidebook to Chicago. "Got it!" she said. She began paging through it. "Here it is," Bess announced a few moments later.

"From the address, I'd say Whitney's is about

33

THE NANCY DREW FILES

three blocks from Reverb," Bess said. "It's even on the same street."

The girls quickly found it, and Nancy was lucky enough to find a parking spot less than a block from the restaurant. A few minutes later, the girls were standing under the huge white awning in front of Whitney's.

"This place sure has a different feel than Reverb," George commented as they walked up the long deep-purple carpet leading to the door of the restaurant. The entire facade was white tile. The restaurant's name was written on the front window in swirling silver letters.

Inside, the atmosphere was just as light and elegant. The effect of the white walls and white wicker furniture combined with enormous flower arrangements and purple tablecloths was striking.

The girls were greeted by a beautiful blond woman who looked as if she could be a model. As she was leading them to their table, Nancy spotted Whitney sitting with another woman at a small table near the kitchen. Excellent! Nancy thought.

Nancy gently touched George's arm.

"I'm going to try to talk to Whitney," Nancy whispered to her friend. "You and Bess go on to our table."

George nodded, following Bess and the hostess to a table against the wall.

As Nancy crossed the dining room, the sound of Whitney's voice reached her. Nancy could tell from her tone that she was angry, and as Nancy slowly approached Whitney's table, the woman's words became clear.

"Nothing would make me happier than seeing Adam's place flop!" Whitney was saying as Nancy walked up to the table.

"What do you want?" Whitney asked coldly when she noticed Nancy standing there.

"My name is Nancy Drew, and I'd like to ask you a few questions."

"Sorry, no," Whitney replied immediately.

"But I—" Nancy started.

Whitney snapped her fingers, and before Nancy could say another word, a huge man came out of the shadows and stepped between her and Whitney. "Ms. Washington would like you to leave," the man said firmly. "Don't make me tell you again."

Nancy met the bodyguard's gaze. She quickly estimated that he outweighed her by at least a hundred pounds.

"But you didn't say 'please,'" Nancy told him.

Anger flashed in the bodyguard's eyes. He took a step toward her, a menacing look on his face.

Chapter

Four

THE BODYGUARD REACHED for Nancy's arm.

Nancy deftly stepped out of his reach and spun slightly to face him, waiting for his next move.

By now most of the diners in the restaurant were watching to see what would happen next, including Whitney Washington herself. At least now I've got her attention, Nancy thought.

The bodyguard's eyes narrowed. "I'm done messing with you, missy," he said, his voice low and gravelly. "This is the last time I'm going to tell you. Leave now or things are going to get ugly."

Nancy felt a firm hand on her shoulder. She turned around quickly, half expecting another beefy bodyguard to be standing there. But instead she found herself face-to-face with George.

"The menu here looks really boring," George

told Nancy. "What do you say we go someplace else?"

"Fine by me." Nancy casually backed away from the guard. Then she turned and walked after her friends toward the door.

The guard followed.

"Now, that's what I call friendly service," Bess quipped as they exited the restaurant.

"No joke!" Nancy answered. She briefly turned and saw the bodyguard standing under the awning, arms crossed, watching them.

"Why did Whitney throw us out?" George asked. "Did you say something to insult her?"

"No," Nancy said. "That's the strange part."

"Maybe she just didn't like the looks of you," George suggested.

Nancy shrugged good-naturedly. "That's about the best explanation I can come up with. She didn't even give me a chance to tell her what I wanted."

"Well, what I want is something to eat," Bess grumbled. "We've been to two restaurants and haven't had any food." She turned to Nancy. "Should we look in the guidebook?"

Nancy glanced at her watch and groaned. "It's almost midnight! How does room service sound?"

"That sounds just about perfect!" Bess exclaimed. "Let's go!"

The next morning the phone rang while Nancy was still in bed.

"I'll get it." George hurried into the bedroom from the bathroom where she had been brushing her teeth. She picked up the receiver. "Hello?"

Nancy sat up in bed and saw that Bess was still asleep. She threw her pillow at Bess's head, and Bess stirred slightly.

"Hi, Frank," George said happily. "No, you didn't wake me. But I can't say the same for my lazy friends."

Bess sat up and rubbed her eyes. "I'm awake," she protested.

"Hold on, I'll ask them," George said. She covered the phone with her hand. "Frank's inviting us to brunch at Reverb. Do you want to go?" Say yes, she mouthed.

"Sounds great," Bess agreed.

"Yes, and I'd also like to tell Adam about what happened last night," Nancy said.

"We'll be there in about an hour," George told Frank.

"Make it an hour and a half," Nancy corrected her. "I want to make a stop on our way."

"Sorry, Frank," George said into the phone. "Could we make that an hour and a half? Okay, see you then!"

George hung up the phone and then just sat on the edge of the bed, grinning.

Bess and Nancy exchanged amused glances.

"What are you so happy about?" Bess asked.

George sighed. "Frank is so sweet. He said that seeing me was going to make his morning."

Bess laughed as she got out of bed. "George, you're beginning to sound like me."

"True!" Nancy exclaimed. "But I don't blame you, George. Frank does seem like a great guy."

"So hurry up and get ready! I don't want to wait all day for you two lazybones."

"Hey, Nancy, what's the stop you want to make?" Bess asked as she crossed the room to the closet.

"I want to stop by the police precinct in this area," Nancy explained. "An old buddy of Dad's is a sergeant with the Chicago police, and I think he's assigned to a precinct near here. I'm hoping he'll be willing to do a favor for me."

Bess and Nancy showered and dressed quickly. A little over an hour later, the three of them were walking into the crowded squad room at a Chicago police station.

"Where could I find Sergeant Chang?" Nancy asked a uniformed officer who was working on a computer near the door.

"He's—"

"Nancy Drew! What on earth are you doing here?"

Nancy looked up and saw her father's friend striding toward her, his arms open wide. "Hi!" she called.

He wrapped her in a hug, then stepped back and beamed, obviously delighted to see her.

"What are you doing in Chicago? Is Carson with you?" Sergeant Chang asked.

"No," Nancy said. "My friends and I are here on vacation—and a case."

"Oh! Well, if this is business, you'd better come into my office," Sergeant Chang said, gesturing toward a tiny glassed-in space. "Follow me, ladies."

Nancy, Bess, and George followed Sergeant Chang into his cramped but tidy office. Once seated, Nancy introduced her friends, then told the sergeant about the happenings at Reverb the night before.

"So, what can I do to help?" Sergeant Chang asked.

"I was hoping you'd be willing to run some background checks on the staff at Reverb," Nancy said.

"Sure thing," Sergeant Chang said. "Do you have the names with you?"

"No," Nancy admitted. "But I'll probably be able to fax them over to you later."

"Sounds good," Sergeant Chang agreed. "Give me a call tomorrow and I'll let you know what we find."

"Thanks." Nancy got up and gave him a quick hug.

"Why do you want to run checks on the staff?" Bess asked Nancy as they headed back toward the car. "Do you think one of them set the smoke bombs?"

Nancy shrugged. "I don't really have a theory yet. But I want to gather as much information as possible. You never know where you'll find a critical piece of information."

"Table for three?" the hostess asked them.

"I'll seat this party!" a male voice replied before the girls had time to speak.

Nancy looked up, expecting to see Frank. Her heart skipped a beat when she saw that Adam was striding toward them.

"It's great to see you, girls," Adam said. But his eyes were focused on Nancy alone.

George, noticing that Nancy seemed flustered, said, "Frank suggested we come by for brunch."

"What a brilliant idea," Adam said. "Remind me to give that Frank a raise. We have the best table in the house waiting for you. Follow me." Adam put his hand on Nancy's arm to steer her to the table.

Nancy felt somewhat dazed. Adam wasn't exactly her type, but she couldn't ignore the way her heart raced at his touch.

"Check out all of the people," Bess said as the foursome crossed the restaurant. All of the tables, except for the one toward which they were heading, were already full.

Nancy knew why her friend was surprised. The front page of a Chicago paper that morning had featured a story about the previous evening's incident at Reverb. One would have thought that the article would have kept people away from the restaurant.

"I thought it was important that we get some good publicity after last night," Adam explained. "So I called a local radio station and told the morning announcer that I was going to play and sing a few numbers at brunch this morning."

"That's smart," George commented.

"Thanks. That's why they call me 'Boss,'" Adam said with a laugh.

They reached the table, and the girls took their seats.

"I need to get back to my office," Adam told them. "A reporter from *Rolling Stone* is supposed to call me in about two minutes."

"I have some news about the case," Nancy said.

Adam raised his eyebrows. "Already? Tell me."

Nancy glanced behind Adam. Almost all of the people in the restaurant were watching him. Not exactly the best place for a private discussion.

"I wouldn't want you to miss your interview," Nancy said smoothly. "Why don't we talk later in your office?"

"Good idea." Adam leaned close to Nancy so that his lips brushed against her hair. "That way we can be alone," he whispered in her ear. Goose bumps rose on Nancy's arm.

Adam headed off toward the kitchen, passing Frank on his way out.

"Good morning," Frank said heartily as he approached their table. "Thanks for coming. I have your breakfast all planned. I've got something special in mind."

"I'm sure whatever you make will be great," George replied.

Nancy and Bess quickly nodded their agreement.

"Okay," Frank said. "I'll get to work, then."

For the next half hour, Nancy thought of nothing but the delicious food that was set before her. The waitress brought out tiny glasses of fresh mango juice and a basket of mini muffins of different kinds, followed by waffles topped with various fruits and yogurt. They finished with oversize cups of frothy cappuccino.

Frank came out of the kitchen to check on them just as the last of the dishes were cleared from their table. "How was everything?" he asked.

"Incredible," George told him, leaning back in her chair with an "I'm full" sigh.

"That was probably the best breakfast I've ever had," Nancy added.

Bess groaned. "I think I gained ten pounds."

"That's okay," Frank teased her. "I hear solving mysteries really burns calories."

"Speaking of mysteries," Nancy said, "it's time for me to get to work. Where can I find Adam?"

"He's in his office," Frank said. "But before you see him, why don't I give you a little tour of the kitchen?"

"That sounds great," George said eagerly.

"Just as long as you don't offer us anything else to eat," Bess added.

"That's a promise," Frank said.

Frank led the girls back to the kitchen, which was swarming with workers dressed in chef's whites. Nancy quickly scanned the room for Paula and was relieved when she didn't spot her. But she did notice another familiar face: Meghan, the pastry chef, was working at a large blender. Spatters of the dough were on the floor near the mixer.

"Hi, Meghan!" Bess called out.

"Hey!" Meghan replied, giving them a welcoming smile.

"What are you making?" Nancy asked.

"I'm *trying* to make angel food cake," Meghan said. "But it's practically impossible to get it right with all of this humidity."

"Well, good luck," Bess said, leaving Meghan to her angel food dilemma.

"I'll tell Adam you're here," Frank told Nancy. He poked his head into Adam's office. "He's still on the phone," Frank reported. "But I told him you were waiting. He'll come out in a second."

Nancy nodded, secretly happy for an excuse to check out the scene in the kitchen. She noted the details she had missed the evening before. Most of the worktables in the cavernous room were made of stainless steel. Oversize pots and pans were stacked on the open shelves underneath.

"What smells so good?" George asked Frank.

44

She stood on her tiptoes so that she could peek into an enormous soup pot.

"Pumpkin soup," Frank told her.

"Really?" George asked. "I don't think I've ever tried that."

"You should," Frank told her. "It's pretty great, if I do say so myself."

"What else are you making?" George asked.

"I'll show you," Frank said.

They wandered down to the far end of the kitchen.

"Things between them seem to be going well," Bess whispered, nodding toward Frank's and George's backs.

"I know," Nancy agreed. "I'm happy for George."

"Well, things seem to be going pretty well for someone else, too," Bess said, stepping aside to let a kitchen worker hurry by.

"What do you mean?" Nancy asked.

"I mean it seems as if you could have a rock star boyfriend, if you want one," Bess said.

"Oh, I don't know about that," Nancy said. But she couldn't look Bess in the eye.

"Adam's been flirting with you ever since he met you," Bess said, her voice rising slightly.

Meghan glanced toward Nancy and Bess.

"He wasn't flirting with me," Nancy insisted.

"Yes, he was," Bess said in a singsong voice.

"Even if he was, I don't think you should get too excited about it," said a person behind Nancy.

Nancy turned and discovered Meghan standing right behind her.

"I'm really not all that excited about it," Nancy insisted.

"Good," Meghan said. "Adam meets hundreds of girls every year. They're always following him around like lost puppies. No offense, but just because he flirts with you doesn't mean he's going to be your boyfriend."

"Here comes trouble," Bess whispered while Nancy was trying to figure out how to respond.

Nancy glanced up and saw Paula bearing down on them. She did not look happy.

"If you people don't mind, my staff has a lot of work to do," Paula said sharply.

"We weren't—" Bess began to protest.

Nancy put her hand on Bess's arm. "Sorry," she said to Paula. "It won't happen again."

Nancy was relieved as Meghan went back to her cake. Bess's teasing and Meghan's pointed comments had been embarrassing. Besides, she needed to concentrate on the case. She spotted an employee schedule tacked up on a bulletin board, went over to it, and began to copy it down. Anything that helped her understand how Reverb operated could be useful.

The moment Nancy finished writing, Adam emerged from his office. He headed directly for Nancy. "Ready for our talk now?" he asked, giving her a warm smile.

"Sure," Nancy said, trying not to appear as

flustered as she felt. She walked with him toward his office.

When they got there, Paula was standing in front of the door. "Where do you think you're going?" she demanded of Adam.

"Peru." Adam rolled his eyes. "Come on, Paula, let me into my office."

"Fine," Paula said tersely. "Just don't forget that you have a hundred fans out there waiting for you to perform."

"If they're really fans, they'll wait," Adam said.

Nancy turned to Adam. "You should go on and perform. Our talk can wait another hour."

"Okay, you win," Adam said to Paula. "Why don't you find Nancy a good seat, Paula? That is, if she's interested."

"Of course I'm interested," Nancy said with a laugh. Who wouldn't want to catch a free concert by a famous musician?

A few minutes later, Bess, George, and Nancy were sitting in folding chairs that had been set up near the small elevated stage at the front of the restaurant. In the short period of time they had been in the kitchen, dozens more people had crowded into the restaurant. The room was buzzing with anticipation.

"I guess that radio station really got the word out," Nancy whispered to her friends.

"Frank said a big crowd is gathered outside," George told them.

Suddenly Adam stepped nonchalantly onto the stage, and the audience burst into applause. "Hi," he spoke into the microphone, and the applause swelled.

"This is so cool!" Bess whispered as Adam picked up a brilliant red electric guitar. He played a chord, then frowned slightly and took a step toward an amplifier.

Adam twisted a dial and then strummed the guitar again. But he still didn't seem satisfied. He stepped back toward the amp. This time, he touched another one of the dials, and there was a loud popping sound. Sparks flew in all directions. The crowd gasped as a bolt of electricity threw Adam backward across the little stage. He landed on his back.

A woman seated in front of Nancy screamed, and the crowd surged to its feet. Amid all the commotion, Adam lay motionless on the stage.

Chapter

Five

THE AUDIENCE stood in stunned silence, and for a moment no one moved. Nancy rushed onstage, followed by George and Bess.

"Is he okay?" George asked as Nancy leaned over Adam.

"He's unconscious," Nancy reported. "But he's still breathing." She started taking his pulse.

"What do you think happened?" George asked.

"It looks as if he got a jolt of electricity from the amp," Nancy guessed. "Maybe it shorted out."

Nancy looked up at George. "Call nine-one-one. I'll stay here with Adam until the ambulance arrives."

"Sure thing." George bolted off the stage to get to a phone.

"What can *I* do?" Bess asked.

"Keep the crowd back," Nancy suggested. "Get some of the waiters to help you."

"No problem," Bess said.

The audience was easy for Bess to manage. Most of the diners were standing in small groups, quietly watching and waiting to see if Adam was okay.

Just then Paula came rushing onto the stage, her face pale. "Is he . . . dead?" Her voice was weak.

Nancy checked Adam's pulse again. "No, his pulse is still strong," she reassured Paula.

Nancy thought the manager seemed genuinely concerned about her boss. But Nancy hadn't forgotten that it was Paula who had encouraged Adam to go onstage and perform. Perhaps she had wanted him to begin playing before someone discovered that the amp had been tampered with. Nancy decided not to leave Adam's side until the ambulance arrived. She was sitting next to him when she heard him groan.

"I think he's coming around," Paula whispered.

Nancy took Adam's hand and gave it a reassuring squeeze. "Everything is fine," she said.

"Where—" Adam mumbled as he opened his eyes. "What the—" He looked around, obviously confused by where he found himself. Then he struggled to sit up.

"Don't move," Nancy said, gently pushing him back down. "The ambulance is on its way."

"Ambulance?" Adam repeated, his voice gaining its usual strength. "I don't need an ambulance!"

"We'll let the medical attendants decide that," Nancy said. "You got a nasty jolt of electricity. You may have internal burns."

Adam turned his head and looked out toward the restaurant, where Bess and several waiters were encouraging the concerned crowd to leave.

"What're they doing?" Adam demanded of Paula. "I don't want this place cleared, do you hear me? We can't afford another fiasco like last night's."

"But surely you don't want these people hanging out while you're examined," Nancy asked. "You'd be on the cover of all the tabloids tomorrow."

"No kidding," Adam said, shaking off Nancy's hand and sitting up. "Listen, if you insist on my being checked out, fine. But the EMS attendants will have to do it in my office."

Before Nancy could stop him, Adam struggled to his feet. "And let the people stay," he told Paula. "And give everyone a complimentary beverage," he added as she hurried off to talk to the waiters.

Bess caught Nancy's eye, and Nancy shrugged. Once Adam was sure the customers weren't leaving, he left the stage and slowly walked through the restaurant toward his office. Nancy followed him.

"So, what did you find out about the smoke bombs?" he asked, as he sat down gingerly at his desk.

"I can't believe you want to talk about the

smoke bombs when you were nearly electrocuted!" Nancy exclaimed. Still, she decided,
maybe it would give him something else to think
about until the ambulance arrived. So she
quickly filled Adam in on the not-so-welcome
reception Whitney had given her the evening
before. She also asked him for a list of employees
to fax to Sergeant Chang. By the time the uniformed medical attendants appeared in the office
doorway, Paula had delivered the list to Adam's
office and the pages were slowly snaking through
his fax machine.

The attendants looked nervous as they started
to pull out their equipment. One man's hands
shook a bit as he unwrapped the blood-pressure
sleeve. He couldn't stop staring at Adam. Nancy
felt a surge of sympathy for Adam. Being famous
had always seemed as if it would be great fun.
But now she realized that being instantly recog-
nizable had a price. She couldn't imagine what it
would be like if everyone she met got so nervous
in her presence.

"So, do you think Whitney was responsible for
today's incident?" Adam asked as his blood
pressure was measured.

"Hard to say," Nancy admitted. "But my gut
feeling is that it's unlikely. Whitney wasn't
around today so she couldn't have tampered with
the amp personally. Of course, she could have
hired someone to do it for her. I'll see what I can
find out."

The attendants finished the exam and began returning the equipment to their bags.

"See, I told you I was fine," Adam said to Nancy.

One of the attendants cleared his throat. "Actually, Mr. Sledge, your heartbeat sounds a bit irregular. It's not at all unusual after a blast like you took. But a heart specialist should check you out immediately. We'll drive you to the hospital."

Adam waved his hand impatiently. "I'll make an appointment with a specialist soon."

"I'm afraid I can't leave it at that," the attendant said rather emphatically. "The first twenty-four hours after receiving a large dose of electricity are the most dangerous. You'll probably need to spend the night in the hospital for observation."

"Oh, all right," Adam said impatiently. He scooped his cellular phone off his desk and followed the attendants back through the restaurant, barking orders in all directions every step of the way. Nancy made sure Adam actually got into the ambulance, and then she went back into the restaurant to find her friends.

"Nan!" Bess called from a small table where she was sitting with George, waiting for Nancy.

Nancy crossed the restaurant.

"How's Adam?" George's concern showed in her eyes.

"Judging by how grumpy he was when he left here, I think he'll be just fine," Nancy said.

"So do you think someone messed with the amp?" George asked.

"I don't know what to think," Nancy said moodily. "It's not too difficult to tamper with the wiring on a piece of equipment like that. But why? And when would someone have done it?"

"I know what *I* think: I think you need a break from this place," Bess said. "Why don't we go shopping?"

Nancy considered Bess's suggestion for a moment. "Sounds like a good plan," she said. "After all, we *are* here on vacation. And it might clear my head."

"We could check out Water Tower Place," George suggested.

"Great," Nancy agreed. "Let's go."

About half an hour later, the trio were strolling through the enormous vertical mall lined with shops. George bought a tennis skirt, and Bess picked up a pair of strappy sandals. Nancy tried to be good company to her friends, but her mind kept drifting back to the case. Was the glamorous Whitney Washington really sabotaging Reverb? For some reason, Nancy found that hard to believe. But if not Whitney, then who?

"Let's stop for something to drink," Bess suggested after they had checked out most of the stores. "I need to sit down."

"There's a coffee shop," George pointed out.

Nancy grabbed a table at the back of the shop while Bess and George went to the counter. A few minutes later, they were settled in with coffees.

"You've been quiet all afternoon," Bess said to Nancy. "Have you figured out anything on the case?"

"Not really," Nancy admitted. "But I don't think that Whitney is our best suspect."

"Even after the way she treated you last night?" Bess asked.

Nancy nodded.

"Do you suspect someone else?" George asked, sipping her coffee.

"Yes," Nancy said. "Paula."

Bess frowned. "She *is* kind of tense."

"Really?" George put in. "I hadn't noticed that."

"You haven't noticed much except for Frank," Bess told her.

"That's not fair!" George exclaimed. But after a moment's thought, she reconsidered. "I guess I *have* been a bit distracted."

"Don't sweat it," Nancy told her friend. "I wouldn't want a mystery to get in the way of true love."

"I think I can handle both," George said. "What makes you suspect Paula?"

"Access," Nancy said. "Since she works almost nonstop at the restaurant, it would have been easy for her to get to the amp and to plant the smoke bombs."

"But why would Paula want to do anything to harm Reverb?" George asked. "If the place goes out of business, she'll end up on the unemployment line."

"That's the same thing that's bothering me," Nancy said.

"Maybe Paula does have a motive, and we just don't know what it is," Bess suggested. "We really don't know anything about her personal life."

Nancy took the last sip of her coffee and stood up. "Well, I say it's about time we find out about it. Let's go check out Paula's apartment. If she's there, we can ask her some questions about this morning. And even if she's not home, we still might learn something."

"Won't she still be at work?" Bess asked.

Nancy opened her notebook to the page on which she had written the Reverb work schedule. "Paula started work this morning at seven," she told the others. "She should finish for the afternoon in about half an hour."

"Maybe we should wait awhile," George suggested. "Give her time to get home."

Nancy considered. "No, let's go now. If she isn't home yet, we can snoop around in peace."

"How will we find out where she lives?" Bess asked, picking up her shoulder bag.

"Wouldn't Adam have her address?" George asked.

"Probably," Nancy said. "But he's in the hospital, remember? Let's try a phone book."

"That's too easy!" George exclaimed.

"It's worth a try," Nancy said. "Why don't you both stay here and finish your coffee? I'll go find a phone book and come right back."

A few minutes later, Nancy returned to the

little coffee shop, triumphantly waving a slip of paper. "I got it!" she called. "I didn't recognize the street name, so I also picked up this map of the greater Chicago area. Paula lives in a suburb about fifteen miles out of town."

Bess and George gathered their packages, and they returned to Nancy's car. Soon Nancy was pulling off a highway exit near Paula's house. The map she had bought turned out not to be much help, and the girls finally had to stop and ask directions to Sullivan Street. Soon after that, they pulled up in front of a modest apartment complex. It was laid out much like a motel, and they climbed an outdoor staircase to Paula's apartment. Nancy couldn't help but feel a bit surprised that Paula lived in such an ordinary building. She dressed so well that Nancy had imagined she would live in an elegant high-rise downtown.

Nancy stepped up to the apartment door and knocked loudly on it. She was startled when Paula threw open the door.

This is what Paula wears when she's hanging out at home? Nancy wondered. Paula was impeccably dressed in slim black trousers and a perfectly ironed blouse. Her hair was sleek and shiny. The only thing off about Paula's appearance was the sour look that came over her face when she saw Nancy standing on her doorstep.

Paula immediately stepped out of the apartment and closed the door behind her. "What are you doing here?" she asked sharply.

Nancy pretended not to notice Paula's tone of

voice. "We came by to ask you a few questions," she said. "Why don't we go inside?"

"Sorry, no," Paula said firmly.

"Why not?" Nancy asked.

"If you must know, I don't want you to disturb my roommate," Paula replied. "She's taking a nap."

"In the middle of the afternoon?" Bess asked.

"She's sick," Paula said. "Not that it's any of your business. Is there anything else you'd like to know?" she added, glaring at Nancy.

What Nancy had already learned was important: Paula was hiding something. She didn't buy the manager's story about the sick roommate for a second. Especially since she could hear voices coming from inside the apartment. Unless her roommate talked in her sleep, Paula was lying.

"Did you see anyone near the amp this morning?" Nancy asked.

Paula shrugged. "Sure, lots of people. Adam hired a crew of guys to set up."

"Did you see anything suspicious?" Nancy asked.

Paula rolled her eyes. "No. If I had seen anything I would have told you."

Nancy seriously doubted that. Paula had made her feelings about Nancy's investigation painfully clear. Nancy knew she wouldn't do anything to help her.

"Maybe later you could get me the names of those guys who were in the crew?" Nancy asked.

"Yeah, sure," Paula said. "Whatever."

"Well, thanks for your help," Nancy said. "We'll get going now. I hope your roommate feels better."

"Gee, thanks," Paula said. She stood outside her door and waited until Nancy, Bess, and George had gotten back into Nancy's car.

"I can't stand that woman!" Bess exclaimed as soon as the girls were on the road again.

"I didn't like her much either," Nancy agreed. "I wonder what she could be hiding."

"Well, we'll have to figure that out tomorrow," Bess said, glancing at the car clock. "We have just enough time to go back to the hotel, change, and get to the jazz club before the first set."

"You're right," Nancy said. The girls had made reservations at the famous Blue Devil club before they'd even left River Heights. Bix Patterson, whose nickname was "the Granddaddy of Jazz," was making a rare appearance. Nancy had been looking forward to the evening for months.

"I wanted to talk to you guys about our plans for this evening," George said, leaning forward in the backseat.

"You should definitely wear your cobalt blue dress," Bess said.

George laughed slightly. "That's not what I wanted to discuss," she said. "Frank isn't working tonight, and when he was showing me around Reverb, he asked me out to dinner. Would you be upset if I skipped out on our plans for tonight?"

Nancy glanced at George in the rearview mirror. "If you're willing to miss Bix to go out with

Frank, well, a girl's gotta do what a girl's gotta do."

"Actually, it was a really easy choice," George said with a shy grin.

"Then go, definitely," Bess told her.

"There's just one problem," Nancy said. "I was planning to go back to Reverb after hours tonight and do some snooping when nobody's around. Can you meet us there, George?"

"Sure," George agreed. "We were planning on an early night. Frank has to get up at the crack of dawn to go to the farmers' market and do the shopping for the restaurant."

"What do you think we'll find at Reverb?" Bess asked.

"I'm not sure," Nancy said. "I'm thinking that maybe something on Paula's desk will suggest a motive."

"I could be there by midnight," George said. "But it might still be open then," she pointed out, "and you said you wanted to snoop around after hours."

"You're right," Nancy said. "Since it's Saturday, the restaurant might be open late." She paused, thinking. "Tell you what," she said after a minute. "Let's meet at midnight anyway, and if the restaurant's still open, we'll just hang around outside until they close up."

"But how will we get in?" George asked.

"I thought I'd stop by the hospital later to get a key from Adam," Nancy said.

4

2

Skipping a Beat

"Where's Frank going to take you?" Bess asked, changing the subject.

"He wouldn't tell me," George said. "He just promised that it would be romantic."

"Wow," Bess said. "What are you going to wear?"

"Something casual," George said. "Frank isn't a black-tie kind of guy."

Twenty minutes later Nancy pulled into their hotel's underground garage. The girls took the elevator to their floor.

"Do you guys mind if I shower first?" Bess asked as Nancy unlocked the door to their room. "It takes a long time to dry my hair."

"No problem," Nancy said.

"Fine with me, too," George agreed. She flipped on the lights.

"Great," Bess said, putting her shoulder bag down on the nightstand. "I'll be quick." She grabbed her robe out of the closet and kicked off her shoes. Then she crossed the room to the bathroom.

George turned on the television and flopped down on her bed, while Nancy went to the closet to pull out her dress.

Both girls jumped when Bess let out a chilling scream.

Chapter

Six

BESS?" Nancy slowly pushed open the bathroom door. "Bess, are you okay?"

George and Nancy stepped into the large, tiled bathroom. "Look at that!" Bess said in a horrified voice, pointing to the mirror. Someone had written in bloodred lipstick over the glass: Go home, Nancy Drew, or you won't be so cute anymore!

In a very low voice Nancy said, "We'd better check out the room to be sure no one's hiding here." The three girls quickly checked under the beds, inside the closet, and behind the draperies for intruders.

"Well, at least no one's in the room now," Nancy said.

"That's good," George said. "But how could

someone have gotten in here to leave that little valentine?"

Nancy shrugged. "It probably wasn't that difficult. Lots of people have access to hotel rooms—the front-desk clerks, maids. But don't let it worry you too much. The room is much more secure when we're in it because we can double-lock the door from the inside."

"Good idea!" Bess exclaimed, running over to check the door.

Nancy went back into the bathroom, where she carefully examined the lipstick used on the mirror.

"What are you doing?" George asked as she and Bess hovered in the doorway.

"Examining our first real clue in this case," Nancy said, sounding almost pleased. "Hand me a tissue, would you? I want to get a smear of this lipstick."

George pulled out a tissue from a box in the wall and handed it to Nancy, who carefully wiped some color onto it.

"Nancy," Bess said, sounding aggravated, "I think you're missing the big picture here. This message means you could be in serious danger. Aren't you even going to consider backing off?"

"Of course not," Nancy said as she carefully folded the tissue.

"Do you really think we can track down that lipstick color and its owner?" George asked. "Thousands of lipsticks are sold every day. It doesn't seem like much to go on."

"You're right," Nancy agreed. "But there's another clue in the message. It says 'or you won't be so cute anymore.'"

"So what?" Bess asked.

"Well, that's the exact word Adam used to describe me at our first meeting, remember?" Nancy asked.

George nodded. "That's right."

"I don't think that's a coincidence," Nancy said. "And that throws suspicion on everyone who was at that meeting."

"Paula was there," Bess said immediately.

"Right," Nancy agreed.

"Well, besides the three of us, the only other person at that meeting was Adam," George said. "Surely you don't suspect him."

"No," Nancy said with a firm shake of her head. "But you're forgetting someone." Nancy took a deep breath before she added, "Frank."

George's face immediately flushed an angry red. "I can't believe you suspect Frank," George said. Without another word, she left the bathroom.

Bess and Nancy exchanged concerned looks, then immediately followed George into the bedroom. They found her pulling her favorite jeans and a mustard yellow sweater out of a dresser drawer.

"George—" Nancy started.

"Let's finish talking about this later," George snapped. "I'm running late now. If I want to be on time to meet Frank, I have to take a shower and get moving."

"Please don't meet Frank," Nancy said. "I admit that I don't have any evidence against him. But I'd feel a lot better if you postponed your date with him."

"I'm not going to do that," George said flatly, gathering up her clothes and heading for the bathroom.

Bess spoke up. "I agree with Nancy, George."

George spun around. "Then you're both being silly," she said fiercely. "Frank is a sweet, gentle guy. He's definitely not the type to go around threatening people."

"We really don't know him that well," Nancy pointed out quietly.

George sighed. "Your theory doesn't even make sense," she insisted. "What could he possibly gain by harming the restaurant? That would just leave him out of a job."

Nancy shrugged. "You're right about that. But *someone* at the restaurant is behind all this. And you could say the same thing about anyone who works there."

"Listen, both of you," George said, obviously struggling to control her temper. "I appreciate your concern. But I'm a big girl and I've made a decision. I'm going to meet Frank and nothing you can say is going to stop me." With that George swept into the bathroom and closed the door behind her.

"What are we going to do?" Bess whispered to Nancy.

"Go see Bix," Nancy said with a sigh. "I think we have to respect George's decision."

"All right," Bess agreed. "But I don't like it."

"Neither do I."

A few minutes later, George emerged from the bathroom and Bess hurried in to take her shower. Even though George talked with Nancy as she finished getting ready, Nancy could tell that she was still angry. Nancy could only hope that George was right about Frank—and that she would owe George an apology when this was all over.

Bess was still in the shower when George left. Since Nancy had time to kill, she let herself out of the room and rode the elevator down to the lobby. She wanted to talk to the hotel manager, as well as the maid assigned to their floor if she was still on duty. Nancy was hoping one of the hotel employees had seen someone come in or out of their room.

"May I speak to the manager, please?" Nancy asked the clerk behind the desk.

"Sure," he replied. "Is there something wrong with your room?"

"Not exactly," Nancy said. "Is the manager in?"

The desk clerk nodded. "Her office is right down that hall," he said, pointing.

Nancy walked down the short corridor. The

office door at the end was open, so she poked her head in. A trim, middle-aged woman in a blue suit was standing behind the desk inside. She was on the telephone, but she smiled when she saw Nancy. "I'll be with you in a second," she whispered.

"Okay," Nancy replied. She retreated back into the hallway.

A small coffee table and a chair had been placed outside the office. Nancy sat down and aimlessly picked up a brochure about the hotel that was lying on the table. She was reading a restaurant review when a photograph of the hotel staff caught her eye. Nancy gasped when she noticed a familiar face in the second row.

"Thanks for waiting," the manager said as she came out of her office. She extended a hand toward Nancy. "May I help you with something?"

"I, um, I was looking for some extra towels," Nancy said quickly.

"Certainly," the manager replied. "Just let me write down your room number, and we'll send up as many as you like."

"Thank you," Nancy said, following the manager into her office. "Two extra sets would be fine."

The manager looked at her quizzically. "You know you can call our housekeeping service any time you need something like this."

"Oh, I know," Nancy answered. "I only just

remembered I needed towels as I was headed out for a walk." The manager nodded her understanding.

"Room number?" the manager asked.

"It's five-fifty-five," Nancy told her. "It's funny, but I was just looking through one of your brochures while I was waiting, and I think I spotted an acquaintance in your employee photo."

The manager smiled at Nancy as she set down her pen. "Really? Who?"

"Paula, um, I'm afraid I can't remember her last name," Nancy said. "I haven't seen her in years."

"Paula Kass," the manager supplied. "Of course! She used to be our night manager."

"Used to be?" Nancy asked. "Oh, too bad. I thought maybe I'd run into her."

"Sorry," the manager said. "That picture is almost a year old. Paula quit a couple of months ago. She got a better job."

"Have you seen her lately?" Nancy probed. "I'd love to say hi."

The manager shook her head. "She hasn't come back to visit even once. I guess her new job must be keeping her awfully busy."

"I guess so," Nancy said. "Well, thanks again for the towels."

"My pleasure," the manager said.

Nancy rode the elevator back upstairs, pleased with her quick detective work. If Paula had worked at the hotel, she surely knew plenty of employees. How hard could it be for her to get a key to Nancy's room? Or to talk one of her friends into scribbling a threatening message on her mirror?

Nancy was still thinking about Paula when she and Bess arrived at the jazz club about an hour later. She decided to put the case out of her mind, though, and enjoy the music. The girls settled in around a tiny table and gave their orders to the waiter.

"Are we late?" Bess asked.

Nancy glanced at her watch. "Nope. The music isn't due to start for about ten minutes."

"Great," Bess said. "That means we have time to soak up the scene."

Nancy sat back and tried to do just that. The club was so tiny that even the smallish stage seemed to crowd the walls. A lustrous black grand piano took up most of the space onstage. Several simple folding chairs and microphone stands claimed the rest of the space. Nancy scanned the audience. A boisterous group of people speaking a foreign language sat just to their right. Just behind them Nancy spotted a familiar face.

"Look who's here," Nancy whispered to Bess.

Bess turned in the direction Nancy was looking and drew in her breath. "Whitney!"

"I'm going to talk to her," Nancy said, getting to her feet.

Nancy quickly crossed the small room and approached Whitney's table. She braced herself for a cold response and could only hope that her attempt to talk to Whitney wouldn't get her and Bess kicked out of the club. Nancy decided to try a different tack.

"Having a nice evening?" Nancy asked pleasantly, holding a hand out to Whitney. She was sitting at a table for four, but two of the chairs were empty. A middle-aged woman in an elaborate sequined dress was sitting on Whitney's right.

Both of the women returned Nancy's smile. Whitney's expression didn't show any hostility. *Doesn't she remember me from last night?* Nancy wondered.

"Excuse me, but have we met?" Whitney asked politely.

Well, that answers that! Nancy thought. "Actually, we have," Nancy said carefully. "I was at Reverb opening last night."

"Oh, I heard about the smoke bombs," the older woman put in, shaking her head in dismay. "What a terrible thing!"

"It was," Nancy agreed. "Actually, that's why I wanted to talk to you," Nancy said, turning toward Whitney. "I'm a detective, and Adam Sledge has asked me to look into the bombing."

"I remember you now," Whitney told Nancy, narrowing her eyes. "You came to my restaurant last night."

"Yes," Nancy confirmed. "You threw me out."

70

"Whitney!" the older woman exclaimed.

"I'm sorry, Mama," Whitney said, patting the older woman's hand. "I thought she was a reporter."

Nancy was so surprised she burst out in laughter. She thought of her own experience with Brenda Carlton, a reporter who had interfered in more than one of her investigations, and immediately forgave Whitney's behavior. She could imagine how difficult it was for a celebrity to be hounded constantly by reporters.

"I understand," Nancy told Whitney. "I probably would have done the same thing if I were you."

"Why don't you sit down?" Whitney offered.

"Thanks," Nancy said, sliding into a seat. "Did you see anything suspicious at Reverb last night?"

"Suspicious? No . . ." Whitney studied Nancy for a moment. "Did Adam tell you I was behind the smoke bomb?" she demanded suddenly.

Nancy glanced uneasily at Whitney's mother. "Actually, yes," she admitted.

"I told you that man was no good," Whitney's mother said to her daughter through pursed lips.

Whitney sighed, looking almost amused. "Yes, you did, Mama. You told me and told me." Whitney turned to Nancy. "Adam was never very popular in my family," she explained. "It took me a long time to realize they were right. I broke off our engagement a few months ago. Adam didn't like that much. Hurt his ego, I suppose. Anyway, he's done his best to make my life miserable ever since."

Nancy wondered about this new spin on the breakup. Adam had said *he* was the one who had broken off their relationship. She scanned Whitney's face for any uneasiness, any indication that she was lying. But Whitney met her gaze evenly and seemed perfectly serene.

"Why would Adam do that?" Nancy asked.

Whitney shrugged. "Because he's a creep. He treats everyone badly. Why should I have been any different?"

"What do you mean he treats everyone badly?" Nancy asked. He's been perfectly nice to me, she thought.

"Take his fans, for example," Whitney offered. "He refuses to give people his autograph after concerts! Word of that kind of attitude gets around. I'm surprised he has any fans left."

Nancy thought back on Adam's blasé attitude toward the people who had been waiting to hear him play that morning. Perhaps Whitney had a point.

A couple of men approached the table. One was a handsome, powerfully built man about Whitney's age. "Are we interrupting anything?" he asked.

"Not at all," Nancy said, standing up. "I'm the one who's interrupting your evening out. Thank you for talking to me, Whitney. Nice to meet you, ma'am," she said to Whitney's mother.

The women nodded at Nancy and turned their attention to the two men.

Nancy got back to her table just as the musicians took the stage.

"How did it go?" Bess whispered.

"It was interesting," Nancy whispered back. "I'll tell you more later."

Nancy sat back to enjoy the music. She couldn't stop thinking, though, about her conversation with Whitney. She wasn't sure whether to believe what Whitney had told her about Adam's nastiness. Her claims didn't jibe with Nancy's own impressions. Could Whitney have purposefully been misleading her? Well, Nancy was certain about one thing: Whitney didn't like Adam. But that didn't mean she would hurt him.

"That was wonderful!" Bess exclaimed when the set ended.

"Definitely," Nancy said. "It was just what I imagined when I think of Chicago."

The girls paid their check, then made their way through the slow-moving crowd to the door. Bess looked at her watch. "We have an hour and a half to kill before we meet George. It's only ten-thirty now."

"Don't forget we have to run over to the hospital to get that key from Adam," Nancy said.

"Then let's go," Bess agreed.

Twenty minutes later, the girls were turning out of the heavy Saturday-night traffic and into the parking lot of a large hospital. Security inside the hospital was tight, but Adam had put Nancy's name on an approved list of visitors, noting that she should be allowed in at any time.

"I guess big rock stars don't have to worry about their guests sticking to hospital visiting hours," Bess commented as the girls got off the elevator on the fifth floor and started down a dimly lit corridor.

"Being rich and famous does have a few benefits," Nancy agreed.

Suddenly the girls heard shouting coming from a room down the hallway. As they got closer, Nancy looked at the room numbers and realized the shouts must be coming from Adam's room.

"Let's go!" Nancy yelled, and started to run. "I think Adam's in danger!"

Chapter

Seven

Nancy raced to the door of Adam's room and threw it open, hoping to surprise Adam's attacker. In one smooth motion, she ran into the room and assumed a karate stance, ready to strike.

Nancy quickly looked around the room—and immediately felt foolish. Adam was sitting up in the bed. Nancy immediately saw he was in no danger. He looked angry, not afraid.

Adam's agent, Larry Sen, whom Nancy recognized from the Reverb opening, was sitting in a chair next to the bed. He looked angry, too.

Nancy took a deep, calming breath and straightened up, trying to regain some dignity.

"Who are you?" Larry demanded. "I'm going to call Security!"

"Don't bother. She's a private detective," Adam said.

"Did you learn that dramatic entrance from television or something?" Larry asked Nancy dryly.

"I heard Adam yelling," Nancy explained. "I thought he was in danger."

"I hired Nancy to help me figure out what's going on at Reverb," Adam put in.

Larry sighed impatiently. "Really, Adam. Isn't hiring a private detective a bit cloak-and-dagger? If you'd bothered to ask me my opinion, I would have told you I thought it was a stupid idea."

"I didn't ask your opinion because I don't care what you think," Adam told him. "It's none of your business."

There was a knock on the door.

"Come in!" Adam yelled.

The door opened a crack, and Bess practically tiptoed inside. She had waited outside the door so that she could call for help, if necessary. Now her gaze jumped from Adam to Larry to Nancy. "Is everything all right?" she asked.

"No, everything is not all right," Adam said testily. "Larry here thinks he can run my life. And I'm trying to make him understand he's my agent, not my mother."

Larry turned back to Adam, having lost interest in Bess and Nancy. "I'm not trying to run your life," he told Adam coldly. "I'm merely offering you some business advice. Last time I checked, that was my job."

Adam rolled his eyes. "Don't worry about me, Larry. I have no doubt Reverb is going to be wildly successful and extremely profitable."

Bess shot Nancy an uncomfortable look. She nodded toward the door and raised her eyebrows.

Nancy knew Bess was suggesting that they should give Adam and Larry some privacy while they discussed business. Part of Nancy agreed with Bess. But the detective in her knew she might learn something important by eavesdropping. And since Larry and Adam hadn't asked her to leave, she decided to stay put. With a quick shake of her head she signaled that Bess should do the same.

"Well, I don't know how you can be so sure," Larry told Adam. "You don't know anything about restaurants. And so far, you've managed only to smoke out your customers onto the street. And end up in the hospital, of course."

"I know how to make people happy," Adam said, his tone smug.

Nancy had to fight a desire to laugh out loud. She had to admit that her friends' impressions of Adam had been on the mark. He was awfully full of himself.

"You know how to make people happy with your music," Larry argued. "And that's where you should be spending your time and creative energy. Not on creating tonight's pasta special."

"I have nothing to do with the menu," Adam replied coolly.

"You know what I mean!" Larry burst out. "You haven't put out an album in over a year. If one doesn't hit the stores soon, your fans will start deserting you!"

Adam burst into laughter. "Drop the Boy Scout routine, Larry. You couldn't care less about my fans, and you know it. The only thing you're worried about is your commission. And since you don't get one on what I earn at Reverb, you think the restaurant is a waste of my time. Well, I've got news for you, buddy. I make the decisions around here. And if I decide I want to spend the rest of my life in the kitchen, then that's what I'm going to do."

Larry stood up. His face was a brilliant pink, but Nancy couldn't tell if he was angry because Adam had insulted him or because Adam was right about his motivation.

"I'm leaving now," Larry said in a surprisingly controlled tone. "I'll call you tomorrow, Adam."

Adam rolled his eyes. "I can't wait."

Larry picked up his coat and briefcase, said good night to Bess and Nancy, and quietly left.

Bess let out her breath in a rush. "Boy, am I glad he's gone!"

Adam winked at her. "Don't worry. That was no big deal. Just business as usual."

Nancy pulled the chair Larry had been sitting on closer to Adam's bed, then sat down. "That's the way you and Larry usually do business?" she asked incredulously.

Adam shrugged. "Pretty much."

"Larry seemed awfully hostile tonight—especially toward Reverb," Nancy said. "Do you think he might be behind the sabotage?"

"No way!" Adam looked at Nancy as if she was crazy.

"How can you be so certain?" Bess asked.

"Larry is a businessman," he explained. "The only thing he cares about is his bottom line. Thanks to clients like me, that bottom line has been pretty fat lately. Now, why would he want to jeopardize that by sabotaging my little restaurant?"

"To get you back in the recording studio?" Nancy suggested.

Adam shook his head firmly. "If Larry got caught, he'd lose everything. Not just me, but all of his clients. It's just not worth the risk."

Nancy had to admit that Adam had a point. But she also knew that people didn't always commit crimes for logical reasons. More often, they broke the law out of anger or a twisted kind of love. Perhaps Larry was angrier with Adam than he was letting on. Nancy made a mental note to check out the volatile agent. Maybe he had some secrets Adam didn't know about.

Bess glanced at her watch and gave Nancy a pointed look. "We'd better get going, or we'll be late meeting George."

"Hey, where *is* George?" Adam asked. "I thought you guys were the Three Musketeers, you know, joined at the hip."

"She's on a date with Frank," Bess told him.

"Really?" Adam's eyes danced with amusement. "Frank and George, huh? Well, George is a lucky girl—Frank's a great guy."

Nancy was surprised. Frank had made it sound as if he wasn't on very good terms with his boss. But Adam's tone was quite affectionate.

"Speaking of George," Nancy said, "we're meeting her outside Reverb at midnight. I wanted to check out the place when no one's around, to see if I can come up with any clues. I wondered if I could borrow your key so we can get in after hours."

"Good idea," Adam said, and reached into the drawer of the cabinet beside his bed. He pulled out a key ring and took off one key. "This is the key to the front door," he said, handing it to Nancy. Then he took out a pen and notepad and wrote something on it. "And this is the number for the security alarm. It's on the left, just inside the door, and you have to punch in the numbers quickly, or else the police will be there in a flash."

Nancy took the paper and put it and the key ring in her shoulder bag. "Thanks," she said.

Adam started to climb out of bed. "Listen, as long as you're going to Reverb, can I hitch a ride home with you two?"

"What are you talking about? You can't leave—you're under observation!" Nancy exclaimed.

"Too bad," Adam said with a shrug. "It's a free country, and I want out of here. I'm tired of giving blood and signing autographs for the Candy Stripers."

Nancy gave Adam a stern look even though she felt a bit sorry for him. "You'll probably be released tomorrow afternoon. Try to enjoy it. Let the nurses spoil you."

"The nurses hate me," Adam pouted.

"We'll see you tomorrow," Nancy said with a light laugh.

"If you really loved me, you'd sneak me out of this joint," Adam said with a sad-puppy frown.

"Love you?" Nancy replied. "I hardly know you."

"Say the word and I'll work on changing that," Adam said with a grin.

The girls said a quick good-bye and ducked out of Adam's room. Whitney might not like Adam, and Frank might think he was a terrible boss. He might even be arrogant. But, Nancy thought, he sure knew how to flirt!

The girls hopped in Nancy's car and drove to Reverb. Frank's car was parked right in front of the restaurant. When Nancy pulled up, George got out of the car. Frank waved to Nancy and Bess from the driver's seat, beeped his horn, and sped off. Nancy pulled her Mustang into the space Frank had just left, and she and Bess got out of the car.

"Frank sure made a quick getaway," Bess joked as she joined George in front of the restaurant.

"It wasn't a getaway," George said, sounding a

bit irritated. "I told you that Frank has to get up early to shop for the restaurant tomorrow. He said all of the best produce at the farmers' market is gone by five-thirty."

"Sorry," Bess told her. "I was just—"

George waved her hand impatiently. "You don't need to apologize. But let's just drop it, okay?"

"Sure," Bess agreed.

"How was your date?" Nancy asked.

A smile softened George's face. "Wonderful. Frank is so romantic! He took me to the top of the Sears Tower. You should see the view!"

"Did you?" Nancy asked in a teasing tone. "Or were you too distracted?"

George playfully hit Nancy on her arm. "Of course I saw the view! This was our first date."

Nancy was happy that George seemed to have forgiven her for thinking that Frank was a suspect, even though she herself hadn't ruled him out.

Nancy noticed for the first time that the restaurant appeared dark. "Looks like Reverb is closed," she said.

"Yes," George said. "They closed early. Frank checked in with Paula earlier this evening, and she told him that hardly anyone had shown up for dinner. People probably were scared away by the bad publicity. Paula decided to close up early."

"I'm glad," Bess said, stifling a yawn. "Let's start investigating. I'm tired."

"I wonder if Paula told Adam she was closing early," Nancy said. "After the way he acted at lunch today, insisting that people stay even after he'd nearly been electrocuted, well, I don't think he'd like it much."

George shrugged. "All Frank told me is that Paula thought the staff could use a break. They've been pretty shaken up since the smoke bombing."

"I don't blame them for being shaken up," Nancy said, digging in her bag for the key to the restaurant, as well as the number for the alarm system. "But I'm also surprised that Paula would take pity on them."

"Maybe Paula had an ulterior motive in clearing out the restaurant early," Bess said as she and George followed Nancy into the darkened space.

Nancy had been wondering the same thing. "What kind of ulterior motive?" she asked. After turning on a light switch near the door, she punched a series of numbers into the burglar alarm keypad.

"I don't know," Bess said. "It was just a thought."

"So you suspect Paula now?" George asked eagerly.

"Actually, I don't know who to suspect," Nancy admitted with a sigh. She watched the keypad until the red light stopped flashing.

"That thing looks pretty sophisticated," Bess commented.

"I'm not surprised," George said. "Frank told

me that the equipment in here is worth hundreds of thousands of dollars."

Nancy found the light switches for the restaurant and flipped them on.

George gasped.

"I can't believe it," Bess breathed.

Neither could Nancy. All of the expensive guitars that had been hanging on Reverb's walls were gone!

Chapter

Eight

ANOTHER INSIDE JOB, Nancy told herself as she looked around at Reverb's empty walls. Adam's valuable guitar collection had been stolen.

"Bingo!" Bess said. "We were wondering if Paula had an ulterior motive for closing the restaurant early. How does grand larceny sound?"

"Pretty convincing," Nancy said glumly. "But anyone who works here would have known that the restaurant was closing early tonight. Not just Paula."

"But the alarm was still armed when we came in," George pointed out. "The thief must have known how to disarm and reset the alarm. I'd guess the wait staff and dishwashers don't know the code."

"True," Nancy said with a sigh. "Well, let's

take a look around. Maybe the thief left us a clue."

"Shouldn't we call the police?" Bess asked.

"Yes," Nancy said, quickly crossing to the hostess station, where a sleek black phone was sitting on top of that evening's reservation sheet. Nancy couldn't help but notice that the sheet was practically empty. The sabotage is working, she thought grimly as she picked up the phone.

But as Nancy started to phone the police, she hesitated. She reached into her bag and pulled out the number of Adam's hospital room.

"Who are you calling?" George asked. She was standing on a chair, examining a part of the wall where one of the guitars had hung.

"Adam," Nancy told her.

George raised her eyebrows in surprise.

Adam's phone rang only once before he answered. "Yes?"

"Adam, it's Nancy."

"Hey, I'm glad you called," Adam said warmly. "Does this mean you've changed your mind about helping me get out of here? Or did you decide you were ready to get to know me better?"

"Neither," Nancy said seriously. "I'm afraid I have some bad news."

"What's up?" Adam asked, all the playfulness gone from his voice.

Nancy took a deep breath. She dreaded Adam's reaction to what she was about to say.

"Bess, George, and I just got to the restaurant," Nancy started uneasily. "Um, Paula closed early and—"

"She did *what?*" Adam demanded. "How come no one asked me first? I leave that joint for a few hours, and everything falls apart—"

"Adam," Nancy interrupted. "I'm not calling to tell you the restaurant is closed. It's about your guitar collection. It's gone."

Nancy heard a sharp intake of breath on the other end of the phone. But Adam didn't say anything.

"Are you okay?" Nancy asked.

"Those guitars are worth a fortune," Adam said in a strangled voice. "I bought the Hendrix with my share of the money from Void's first album. They can't be gone."

"I'm sorry," Nancy said quietly. "Listen, why don't I hang up now and call you back later? I want to report this to the police."

"No!" Adam said forcefully. "No police."

"Why not?" Nancy asked.

"I don't want any more bad publicity for Reverb," Adam said. "If you call the cops, this will be all over the papers and on TV tomorrow. And then we'll have another big mess to deal with."

"I don't see how we can avoid it," Nancy said. "Tomorrow's brunch crowd is definitely going to notice that something is missing."

"If anyone asks, we'll tell them that we removed the guitars for safekeeping or cleaning or something." Adam laughed harshly. "I just wish it was true."

"That may solve your public relations problem," Nancy said. "But what about getting your property back?"

"Leave that to me," Adam told her. "I know someone who specializes in these kinds of searches. I'll call him right now."

"Well, I guess you're the boss," Nancy agreed reluctantly. She didn't like leaving a crime unreported. But the guitars were Adam's, and so was the restaurant. He had the right to decide how the case should be handled.

"No cops?" George demanded as soon as Nancy had hung up.

Nancy shook her head.

"I don't like that," George said. "What is Adam trying to hide?"

"He's just trying to keep the story from the media," Nancy replied as evenly as she could. George had seemed determined to think the worst of Adam ever since they met him. Her hostility was beginning to bug Nancy.

"There are no clues out here," Bess put in. "Let's move into the back."

"Good idea," Nancy agreed.

The girls trooped into the kitchen. Bess flipped on a light.

"Everything seems to be in place," Nancy commented. She examined the back door very carefully for pry marks or stress of any kind. Nothing.

Bess paused to read some announcements that had been tacked up on a bulletin board for employees.

George wandered into the manager's office, a tiny space divided from the kitchen with glass walls.

Nancy looked in from the doorway. "Find anything in there?"

"No," George said. "It's strange. I know this is Paula's desk because I've seen her working in here during the day. But if I hadn't known that, I'd never guess this was her workplace. It's so sterile. There's absolutely nothing personal here."

Nancy came around the back of the desk and sifted through a tidy stack of papers. "Invoices for the restaurant," she said. "Copies of newspaper stories about the smoke bomb. Completed job applications. Nothing out of the ordinary."

"There's also a to-do list," George noted.

Nancy's gaze drifted to Paula's state-of-the-art computer. Her to-do list was taped to the corner of the monitor. "'Payroll,'" Nancy read out loud. "'New Saturday schedule.'"

Nancy sighed and turned away from the list. "Nothing incriminating there. But then again, I wouldn't really expect Paula **to wri**te 'drive away business' on her to-do list."

George giggled. "I guess not."

"Why don't we see if Paula has any unusual computer files?" Nancy suggested.

"Okay," George agreed. She reached around the back of the computer and switched it on.

While they were waiting for the computer to boot up, Nancy looked through Paula's desk drawers. But all she found inside were files and a well-organized collection of office supplies. "I can't get a handle on Paula," Nancy told George.

George nodded. "She's all business. I mean most people have something personal on their desks. At least a family photo!"

Nancy winked at her. "Maybe Paula doesn't have a family. I'm beginning to suspect that she's an alien."

George snapped her fingers. "That would explain it. You can't put a photo of Mom and Dad on your desk if they have antennae."

"And that green skin is so hard to hide," Nancy added.

Nancy and George were still laughing when Bess hurried into the office, carrying a white chef's coat in her arms. "I think I found something!"

"I'm glad someone has," Nancy said. "What is it?"

Bess turned the coat over to reveal a smear of bloodred lipstick. "Look familiar?" she asked.

"Is that the same color from our bathroom?" George guessed.

"There's only one way to be sure," Nancy said. She opened her bag and fished out the tissue on which she had smeared some of the lipstick from the mirror. She walked under one of the kitchen's bright lights, unfolded the tissue, and compared the smear of color there to the one on the jacket.

"It matches!" Bess said.

Nancy frowned thoughtfully. "That's almost too neat. It's almost as if someone left that coat out for us to find."

But Bess shook her head. "I didn't find it with the rest of the coats. They were folded on a shelf near the bathroom. This one was crammed back behind some pots. Someone was definitely trying to hide it."

"Whose coat is that?" George asked.

"I have no idea," Bess said.

"Some restaurants get their chefs' jackets cleaned with the linens," Nancy said. "They just write the name of the owner inside with a laundry pen."

Bess turned down the collar. Nothing. But when she opened the coat a handwritten name was clearly visible just inside the lapel. Bess drew in her breath sharply when she read what was written there: Frank Cassone.

Chapter
Nine

GEORGE STARED angrily at the chef's coat Bess was still holding. "Don't tell me you guys suspect Frank just because of this!"

Bess dropped her eyes to the floor, but Nancy met George's challenging gaze. "I'm sorry, George," Nancy said quietly. "It's not that I'm convinced Frank is guilty. But at this point, I think we have two main suspects. Paula is one of them. And Frank is the other."

"Come on, Nancy," George argued. "Can't you see that this is a setup? If Frank was guilty, why would he have left that chef's coat at the restaurant? Nobody is that stupid! Plus he wouldn't have been wearing a chef's coat when he wrote that message. And what would he be doing with lipstick anyway?"

"Calm down, George," Bess said in a soothing tone. "Don't take this so personally."

George spun around to face Bess, her face red with anger. "Sorry, but this *is* personal!" George said. "My two best friends think someone I care about is a criminal. How could it get more personal than that?"

"I never said that I thought Frank was guilty," Nancy told George calmly. "And what you said makes sense. Still, some of the evidence does point to him."

"Like what?" George demanded.

"Well, Frank doesn't seem to like Adam," Nancy said.

"Why would he like him?" George said a shade more calmly. "Adam is a terrible boss. He's always losing his temper and threatening to fire Frank."

"That's what Frank told us," Nancy said.

"Why would he lie about something like that?" George demanded.

"I don't know," Nancy admitted. "But tonight Adam told us he thought Frank was a great guy. And he really seemed sincere."

"Ha!" George said, pointing a finger at Nancy. "I think you're the one who's letting your feelings get in the way of your judgment. You're attracted to Adam, he's been flirting with you, and you want to believe he's a nice guy. When Frank tells you he's not, you think Frank is lying."

Nancy felt her own face flush with anger. But

after a moment's reflection, she realized George had a point. Love is blind, as the old saying goes. And even though Nancy wasn't in love with Adam, she couldn't deny the attraction she felt toward him. Maybe that made her a bad judge of his character.

"What do you think?" Nancy asked, turning to Bess. "Was Adam being honest tonight?"

Bess shifted her weight uneasily. "I think so. I'd have to say Adam really does seem to like Frank."

George sighed in frustration. "But it doesn't add up. Don't you think that if Frank was guilty, he'd pretend to like Adam?"

"Maybe," Nancy said. "But some criminals don't bother to cover their tracks very well. And sometimes the most obvious person actually *is* guilty."

"Listen," George said, her mouth tight with anger, "I know Frank better than you do. And you're wasting your time trying to pin this on him. I just know he didn't do it."

"Your opinion is noted," Nancy said with a smile. She stepped forward and tried to give George a hug. But George's shoulders remained stiff. Nancy took a step back. "Listen, I promise to keep an open mind."

"Fine," George said shortly.

Bess and Nancy exchanged concerned glances.

"Maybe we should call it a night," Bess suggested.

"Good idea," Nancy agreed.

The mood was tense as the girls moved around, turning out lights and resetting the burglar alarm. George was quiet on the ride back to the hotel.

"So, tell us more about your date," Bess said lightly. "What did you and Frank do before your romantic trip to the Sears Tower?"

"I'm sorry, Bess," George said. "But I just don't feel like talking about it anymore."

"Okay," Bess said softly.

Since Nancy didn't know what she could say that would make George feel better, she concentrated on thinking about the case. She knew that the sooner she discovered who was sabotaging Reverb—and proved it—the sooner things would go back to normal between her, Bess, and George.

If anything, Nancy felt she had too many suspects: Paula, Frank, Whitney, even Larry. But try as she might, Nancy couldn't convince herself that any of them were guilty. One thing, though, wasn't difficult to figure out: being a famous rock star was no party. As far as she was concerned, the price of fame was way too high.

"How many of these people does Larry Sen currently represent?" Nancy said into the phone the next morning. "Yes, I understand. Okay, well, thank you very much. You've been very helpful."

Nancy was standing next to a bedside table in the girls' hotel room, holding a list of names on fax paper. Bess was sitting on one of the beds, eagerly listening to Nancy's phone call. George was sitting in a chair by a round table, reading. Once in a while, she sighed deeply and turned a page. The girls had already been up for more than an hour, and George had hardly exchanged a word with Bess and Nancy.

"Let me see that list," Bess said as soon as Nancy hung up the phone.

Nancy handed Bess the list and sat down next to her on the bed.

"Wow," Bess breathed.

"That list includes some of the biggest names in rock," Nancy commented.

"And you got home phone numbers!" Bess exclaimed.

"Yeah," Nancy said. She found that a little hard to believe herself. "Dad managed to pull some strings at the Musicians Guild. But I had to promise to use the numbers only for the purposes of this investigation. After that, we have to burn them or eat them or something."

Bess pouted. "If we only get to use these numbers once, then I want to make some of the calls."

"Fine," Nancy agreed. "I'll go downstairs and get us some breakfast. You can get started while I'm gone."

"Great!" Bess jumped up to get a notebook and a pen.

Nancy turned to George. "Want to come downstairs with me?"

"No, thanks," George said coldly.

Nancy held back a sigh. She had hoped that George's anger would pass as the morning wore on. But so far she seemed even angrier.

Bess was punching numbers into the phone as Nancy let herself out the door.

About ten minutes later, Nancy returned to the room with a large paper bag, which she set on the table near George. She took out three cups of orange juice, three cups of coffee, and an assortment of sweet rolls. George looked up from reading but didn't say anything.

"Thanks so much for your help," Bess said warmly into the phone. "Goodbye now," she added before hanging up.

Bess turned to Nancy. "Guess who that was!" she demanded with a broad grin.

"I don't know—who?"

"Amanda Day!" Bess exclaimed.

"Really?" Nancy was impressed. Amanda Day was one of her favorite singers.

"Really," Bess said. "And she was so nice! She even answered the phone herself. Can you believe that?"

"The Musicians Guild probably gave us a number right next to her bed," Nancy said with a giggle. "So what did she say?"

"Say . . ." Bess looked blank for a moment. "Oh, you mean about Larry?"

"Of course!" Nancy exclaimed, shaking her head. "That *is* why you called her, or did you forget to ask about him?"

"No, no, I remembered," Bess said. "But she only had good things to say about him. She said he's a terrific agent. I even asked her if she felt he charged too much."

"And?" Nancy asked.

Bess shook her head. "She said he charged her fifteen percent—the standard in the industry. And she said he was well worth it."

Nancy sighed as she took the top off her cup of coffee. "Well, I guess we just have to keep trying. George, do you want to make the next call?"

George smiled for the first time since the night before. "Who is it?"

Bess consulted the list and named a musician who had been famous years earlier, during the disco era. Her music was making a big comeback.

"Sure, I'll call her," George agreed. "It should make a good story once we get home."

Nancy smiled at George as George stood and walked over to the telephone. She was relieved that her friend was at least talking to her.

After looking at the list, George punched in the phone number. "Answering machine," she said with disappointment. "Should I leave a message?"

Nancy shook her head. "It's probably better if we try again later."

George hung up. "Your turn," she said, handing Nancy the list.

Nancy made the next call, to a well-known jazz drummer who had a regular gig on a late-night talk show. She got the drummer on the phone, but he didn't have much to tell her. Like Amanda Day, he thought Larry was a great agent.

The girls each took several more turns calling the names on the list. But none of the calls turned up anything of interest. All of Larry's clients seemed to like or at least respect him.

"Okay, Bess, it's your turn," Nancy said.

Bess flopped back on the bed. "I can't face talking to one more famous rocker. Let's take a break. Isn't it—"

Just then the phone rang.

"Maybe that's one of Larry's clients calling *us* to tell us how wonderful he is," Nancy said before she answered the phone. "Hello? Oh, hi, Sergeant Chang. You did? Great! Oh, really? Well, I guess that's good news. Thanks."

"What did he say?" George asked when Nancy hung up.

"The background checks turned up zilch," Nancy reported. "Aside from a few unpaid parking tickets, the employees at Reverb are good citizens. No records."

"Now what?" Bess asked.

Nancy shrugged. "I guess it's back to the phones."

Bess sat up and reached for the phone. But before she could pick it up, it rang again.

"Hello?" Bess said. "Yes, she is. Just a second." She covered the mouthpiece with her hand. "It's for you, Nancy. Larry Sen."

Nancy raised her eyebrows and took the

phone. "Hello?" she said. "Oh, I'm sorry. We've been on the phone most of the morning. We were, um, doing a little work on the case. No, Adam isn't here. Shouldn't he still be at the hospital?"

George noticed that Nancy suddenly grew rigid.

"Yes, of course," Nancy said. "We'll go right over."

"What's wrong?" George demanded as soon as Nancy hung up the phone.

"Adam has disappeared!"

Chapter

Ten

W<small>HAT DO YOU MEAN</small> he disappeared?"
George asked.

"Adam wasn't in his hospital room early this morning when a nurse went in to monitor his blood pressure," Nancy explained. "And all his things were gone."

"Well, maybe he just decided on his own to go home," George suggested calmly.

"I thought we had talked him out of that last night," Nancy said. "Anyway, if he left on his own, he didn't go home. Larry went by Adam's house, and his live-in housekeeper hasn't seen him."

"Maybe he's at Reverb," Bess suggested.

Nancy shook her head. "Larry called there and was told that Adam hasn't been there all morning. Larry's on his way to talk to the police. He sounded pretty shook up. He thinks that Adam is dead or has been kidnapped."

"What should we do?" Bess asked.

"Find him." Nancy stepped into a pair of shoes, scooped her car keys off the dresser, and picked up her shoulder bag. "Let's go!"

Nancy, George, and Bess headed down the hospital corridor to Adam's room. Nancy had wanted to see if there was some clue there to Adam's disappearance. The girls hurried into Adam's room. The bed was neatly made. Nancy peeked into the bathroom and the closet, but she didn't see any sign that Adam had ever been there. She looked in the drawers of the bedside table and even under the bed. She found nothing.

"Let's see if we can find a nurse," George suggested.

The girls rushed back down the corridor and stopped in front of the nurses' station.

"May I help you girls?" A dark-haired nurse behind the desk looked up from the chart she had been filling out.

"We're looking for Adam Sledge," Nancy said.

"You and every other young woman in Chicago. Luckily, he left this morning before I came on duty." She rolled her eyes. "Having a celebrity on the floor is nothing but extra work. The phone never stops ringing. And the press is awfully sneaky about getting in. Say, you girls aren't reporters, are you?"

"No," Nancy said impatiently. "We're friends of Adam's."

"I see." The nurse eyed Nancy suspiciously. "Well, then, I guess you can see him at home."

"Adam is missing," Nancy told the nurse. "Isn't there someone who was working last night we can talk to?"

"No, there isn't," the nurse said curtly. "And I'm going to have to ask you to leave now. No reporters are allowed on the floors."

"We're not—" Nancy started.

But Bess put a hand on her arm. "Come on, Nancy, let's go."

Nancy was fuming, but she let Bess and George lead her to the elevator. The doors opened as soon as they pushed the button. A custodian with a mop and a bucket was standing in one corner, and he gave the girls a bright smile as they got into the elevator.

"Remind me never to take another famous client." Nancy leaned over and pushed the button for the ground floor even though it was already lit up.

"We had someone famous here last night," the custodian remarked.

Nancy turned and faced the man. "You were working here last night?"

Under Nancy's intense scrutiny, the custodian lost his open smile. "Y-yes," he replied uneasily. "I mean, I guess so."

Nancy took a deep breath. "Don't worry," she

said soothingly. "You haven't done anything wrong. I just asked because I'm so worried about my friend Adam. He was here last night and now he's missing."

The custodian looked up and studied the floor numbers, which were clicking by slowly. "A *famous* Adam?" he asked.

"Yes!" Nancy said eagerly.

The elevator stopped on the third floor, and several doctors stepped on. The custodian looked down into his bucket. He didn't say another word until the elevator doors opened on the ground floor. After the doctors got off, he leaned forward. "Don't worry about your friend," he whispered in Nancy's ear. "I took care of everything."

"What do you mean?" Nancy asked.

"I called him a cab," the custodian explained.

"Why did you do that?" Bess asked.

"Because he asked me to," the custodian said. "I do that a lot. Some people just don't want to be here. They offer me money to call them a cab. I'm always glad to help. I don't believe people should be here if they don't want to be. Adam gave me a twenty."

"Do you remember what cab company you called?" Nancy asked.

"Of course," the custodian replied. "The number is on that phone over there."

"Thank you," Nancy said.

"No problem," he told her. "Tell Adam I said hello." The custodian started down the hall.

George approached the phone he had pointed

out. She studied the card listing emergency phone numbers. "I think we have a problem," she reported. "There's no cab company number listed here."

Nancy peeked over George's shoulder at the phone. "Maybe he means this," she said, pointing to a small sticker on the side of the phone.

"'Great Lakes Cabs,'" George read. "That must be it." She pulled some coins from her jeans pocket and pumped them into the phone. Then she dialed the number. "Do you want to talk to them?" she asked Nancy.

Nancy took the phone and quickly learned that Adam had been dropped off at Reverb around six o'clock that morning. She sighed as she hung up the phone. "The trail leads back to Reverb," she told her friends.

"Everything bad in this town seems to happen there," George commented.

"Well, we'd better get going," Bess said. "Adam could be in serious danger."

Nancy didn't need to be told twice. She realized just how true Bess's words were. She no longer believed that someone was just trying to close down the restaurant. She suspected that someone was trying to harm Adam. But who? And why?

The girls drove directly to the restaurant and entered through the kitchen door. Inside, it was business as usual. A full kitchen crew was busy preparing brunch.

"I'm going to look for Frank," George announced.

"Great," Bess said to Nancy as George walked out of earshot. "Adam has been kidnapped, and George is going to spend the rest of the morning flirting. Can I do anything useful?"

"The wait staff must be setting up in the dining room," Nancy said; "You can start by asking them if they've seen Adam this morning."

As Bess left, George returned. "Meghan says Frank isn't here."

Nancy frowned. Adam and Frank were both missing. Could Frank have kidnapped Adam?

"Where is he?" Nancy asked George, trying to keep the accusation out of her voice.

"Still shopping," George said evenly. But Nancy could see a flicker of worry in her eyes.

"So, who's in charge when he's not here?" Nancy asked.

"Meghan, I guess," George said.

"Let's go talk to her," Nancy suggested.

Meghan was pouring something into the bowl of a huge whirling mixer. George and Nancy joined her, and Nancy peeked into the bowl.

"What are you making?" Nancy called over the noise of the machine.

When Meghan saw Nancy and George, she turned off the mixer. It stopped instantly, and tiny globs of the mixture splattered out. Nancy and George both jumped back.

Meghan noted their reaction with amusement. "Sorry about that," she said. "This thing's a little messy, but you get used to it after a while."

"What are you making?" Nancy asked again.

"Chocolate mousse," Meghan said. "Only I'm having a hard time concentrating. I'm too worried about Adam to think straight. What do you think happened to him?"

"That's what we wanted to ask you about," Nancy told her. "Have you seen him this morning?"

"No," Meghan said.

"What time did you get in?" Nancy asked.

"We start prep work for brunch around seven," Meghan told her. "This morning I overslept a little and didn't get in until around seven-fifteen."

"Was anyone here before you?" Nancy asked.

"Mitch and Lizzy, two of the prep chefs, were waiting for me outside," Meghan told her.

"Can you point out Mitch and Lizzy to me?" Nancy asked.

"Sure," Meghan said. "That's Mitch over there chopping onions." She pointed to a very tall man with a mass of wavy, salt-and-pepper hair. "And that's Lizzy," she said, indicating a petite Asian woman who was whisking something over the stove.

Nancy made a mental note to question them later. "So you all came in here at seven-fifteen?" she asked Meghan.

"No," Meghan said. "I don't have any keys, so the three of us had to wait for Paula to get here and let us in. That's why we're behind now. She didn't arrive until around seven-thirty."

Nancy and George traded looks. Paula was late to work? That seemed very out of character.

Could she have been delayed because she was somehow behind Adam's disappearance?

"And Adam wasn't here when you came in?" Nancy asked.

"No," Meghan said.

"And was there any sign of—" Nancy started.

"What's going on here?"

Nancy spun around and found herself face-to-face with Paula.

"I'm getting a little tired of you people waltzing in here any time and disturbing my staff," Paula barked. "My staff has work to do. And that doesn't include standing around talking to you."

Nancy suppressed a sigh. Why was Paula always giving her such a hard time? And why did she always look so perfect doing it? Seeing Paula's beautiful outfit made Nancy aware of how casual she herself looked. She was wearing a short denim skirt, a blue T-shirt, and a jeans jacket.

Paula, on the other hand, was perfectly pulled together. She was dressed in an expensive-looking tailored pants suit and a gorgeous pair of black shoes. Although, Nancy noticed with a secret satisfaction, Paula's shoes didn't look too hot. The dark leather was covered with tiny white speckles. I wonder how Paula let that detail slip by her? Nancy thought.

"Larry called to tell us Adam was missing," George told Paula impatiently. "We're here to find him."

"Well, let me help you," Paula replied. "He's not here. Any idiot could see that."

"Nancy!" Bess called from across the kitchen. "I think you'd better get over here."

"What is it?" Nancy asked as she rushed to her friend's side. George followed her.

"I just came back from the dining room, and as I walked past the freezer, I think I heard a thump from inside!"

"Probably just some butter falling off the shelf," Mitch, one of the prep cooks, commented.

"I just heard it again," George said.

Nancy pulled on the freezer door. It wouldn't open. "Is this usually locked?" she demanded.

"Actually, no," Mitch admitted. "It's always been unlocked whenever I've needed to get something."

"Have you been in there this morning?" Nancy asked.

The prep chef shook his head. "That's only used for bulk supplies. Ice. Ice cream. Stuff like that. Most of the food we need is kept in the walk-in refrigerator."

"Who has the key to the freezer?" Nancy asked.

"Frank does, and Adam, too," Mitch said. "I'm not sure who else."

"Paula, do you have a key to this freezer?" Nancy called out.

"Yes," Paula said. She seemed to have decided that the fastest way to get rid of Nancy was to prove Adam wasn't there. "I'll get it." Paula went off to her office, but a moment later she was back. "My key is gone," she reported, looking concerned for the first time.

109

"Meghan!" Nancy called. "Do you have a key for this thing?"

Meghan stared at Nancy wide-eyed and shook her head.

By now the entire kitchen staff had stopped working and was watching Nancy, Bess, and George. Nancy examined the lock. "A crowbar would open this," Nancy said. "Are there any tools around?"

"In the basement," one of the waiters spoke up. "I'll get them."

A few minutes later, Nancy was sorting through the enormous tool box the man had hauled up the steps from the basement. The box didn't contain a crowbar, but Nancy did find a solid chisel with a hollow handle. She wedged the chisel between the door and the doorjamb. Then she fit a broom handle into the chisel handle. George helped Nancy push against the handle until the lock popped.

Nancy yanked the door open and flipped on the light inside. She stepped inside with George right behind her.

"Oh, no," George gasped.

Adam Sledge was slumped down in one corner, his eyelids and lips a deep blue.

Chapter

Eleven

NANCY DROPPED DOWN to her knees beside Adam. She leaned over and held her cheek inches from Adam's face, hoping to feel his breath on her face. Nothing. Nancy's fingers were shaking as she pressed them to Adam's cold neck and searched for a pulse. She looked up at George when she felt a strong beat under her fingers. "He's alive!"

"Then we have to get him warmed up," George said. "Let's get him out of here."

Nancy shivered as she and George each slipped a hand under Adam's arms. He was still wearing the thin Cubs T-shirt he had worn in the hospital, and his skin was cold to the touch. Nancy knew that the temperature in the freezer must be below freezing. She wasn't sure how long he had been in there, but one thing was clear: it was almost too long.

The girls half lifted Adam and half dragged him out of the freezer. Several people rushed forward to help them.

"I can't believe this," Paula whispered, staring at Adam's motionless form.

"Someone get a chair," Nancy said.

Paula snapped out of her trance. "I'll get one out of my office," she offered, rushing off.

"We'll also need some blankets," Nancy said, looking up into the sea of faces that surrounded her. "Or some tablecloths will do."

Meghan's gaze flitted from Nancy's face to Adam's unmoving form. "Do you—is he—he's not dead, is he?" she asked unsteadily.

"No," Nancy said gently. "We just need to get him warmed up. You can help by finding something to wrap him up in."

"I have a blanket in my car," Meghan said. "I'll go get it."

Meghan hurried off. By then Paula had come out of her office with the chair. Nancy and George carefully sat Adam down in it. Soon after, Meghan arrived with the blanket. Nancy wrapped it around Adam tightly. Then she sat down in front of the chair. She took one of Adam's hands and warmed it between her own. "Come on, Adam, wake up," she whispered to him. "Please wake up."

Adam seemed to hear Nancy's plea. Her heart pounded painfully as Adam's eyes opened with a flutter. "Hi, Miss Nancy Drew," he said weakly. "You sure took your time getting here." Adam rolled his head from side to side and let out a low groan.

"Sorry about that," Nancy told him. "We got here as fast as we could."

Bess knelt down next to Nancy. "I think we should call an ambulance," she whispered.

"No ambulances," Adam said, suddenly alert. "I'm not going back to the hospital. I hate that place."

"Adam, you really should," Nancy argued. "Exposure can be very serious. Especially after all you've been through in the past couple of days."

"That's for sure," Adam said. "I was in that freezer so long, I thought I was going to turn into a human Popsicle. I tried to keep myself warm by pacing. But finally, I couldn't stay awake anymore. I must have fallen." Adam gingerly felt the side of his head and his shoulder. "I guess I hit a shelf or two on the way down."

"It's a good thing you did," George told Adam. "Bess heard a thump, and so did I. That's how we found you."

"Earlier, I was banging on the door, but I gave up because I knew no one would be at work for at least an hour. By then I guess I was out of it. So—thanks!"

"You're welcome," she said. "And as a show of your appreciation, why don't you let me call that ambulance?"

"No, thanks," Adam said. "I'm actually starting to feel better."

"Here, Adam, this tea should warm you up," Mitch said as he handed Adam a steaming cup.

Adam accepted the cup and winked at Nancy. "I can think of some more interesting ways to get warm."

Bess caught Nancy's eye and laughed lightly. "Okay, I give in," she said. "No ambulance. This man is showing familiar signs of life. I think he's going to make it."

"Maybe you're even strong enough to explain how you ended up in the freezer," Nancy said. "Did you see who locked you in?"

Adam studied the circle of faces surrounding him. He handed his tea back to Mitch, pushed off the blanket, and stood up. "Come on, I'll tell you detective types all about it in my office. Everyone else, please get back to work. The brunch rush is about to begin."

"Good idea," Paula said approvingly.

"Paula, why don't you come with us?" Adam suggested.

Nancy started to protest. She didn't want Paula to hear what Adam might reveal. But then Nancy decided to let it pass. She felt more certain than ever that Paula was somehow involved with the sabotage, and the more opportunity she had to observe Paula, the better.

Adam walked off toward his office with Paula, Nancy, George, and Bess following. Once inside, he pulled a luxurious black sweater off the back of his chair and shrugged it on.

"Why don't you close the door?" Adam suggested when everyone was inside.

Paula closed the door but stood next to it as if she couldn't wait to get back to work.

Nancy carefully watched Adam for any sign of exhaustion or confusion, which could be lingering effects from exposure. So far he seemed fine. But Nancy decided she would try to talk him into seeing his doctor as soon as she finished getting his story.

"So, what happened?" Nancy prompted Adam after he had gotten settled in his leather chair.

Adam sighed. "Well, early this morning, I got a mysterious call at the hospital. It woke me out of a dead sleep—and interrupted a beautiful dream." He smiled at Nancy.

She gave him a behave-yourself frown. "Who was on the phone?" she asked impatiently.

"I don't know," Adam said with a shrug. "They just told me that if I wanted to see my guitars again I should meet them here at six this morning."

"Why didn't you call me?" Nancy asked angrily.

"The person said to come alone," Adam explained.

Nancy shook her head. "Sounds like something out of a bad movie." She glanced at Paula. "This voice—was it a man's or a woman's?"

"Couldn't tell," Adam said. "It sounded almost mechanical. Like maybe the person was talking through one of those electronic distorters."

"Then what?" Nancy prompted him.

"I bribed the custodian to call me a cab," Adam said.

"That much we were able to find out on our own," Nancy told him. "So what happened after you left the hospital?"

"I took the cab here," Adam said. "I waited outside for about half an hour, but nobody showed. After that, I'd had it. Waiting is not my thing. So I went inside." He shook his head sadly. "Man, I still can't believe all my guitars are missing. The restaurant looks awful. All those empty walls."

"What happened then?" Nancy prompted.

"I heard a voice coming from the kitchen," Adam said. "I went to investigate. The door to the walk-in freezer was propped open, and the voice was coming from inside. That gave me the creeps, but I stepped inside the freezer to see what was going on. The door slammed shut behind me. When I tried to get out, the door was locked."

"But there's an emergency release inside," Paula said. "Surely, you remembered that. We argued at least six times about the extra money it cost."

"I remembered," Adam said. "I didn't think it

was worth the money then and I still don't. The stupid thing didn't work. Someone probably messed with it."

"What about the voice?" George asked.

"There was a tape recorder inside the freezer," Adam told her. "Funny thing is, it was my own voice I was hearing. A tape of my appearance on the *Ira Stein Show.*"

"Where's the tape recorder now?" Nancy asked.

"Still in the walk-in, I guess," Adam said.

"Should I get it?" George asked Nancy.

Nancy nodded, and George left the office.

"Okay," Nancy said, thinking out loud. "Who has keys to the freezer?"

"Excuse me, but—" Bess said.

"Adam, Frank, and me," Paula said. "But my keys are missing."

George came back into the room in time to hear Adam exclaim, "Frank! I bet he did this!"

"Nancy—" Bess started.

"Where is he?" Adam demanded. "I want to speak to him immediately!"

George shot a desperate look at Nancy. Her eyes clearly said "do something!" But at that moment Nancy couldn't worry about protecting Frank. She was distracted by something much more important.

"Excuse me!" Bess said more insistently.

"I'm calling the police," Adam announced, reaching for the receiver.

"Adam, you don't want to do that," George said.

"Yes, I do!" Adam yelled. "I want that guy behind bars!"

But Nancy put out her hand before Adam could dial the phone. "Everyone has to get out of the restaurant now," she insisted. "I smell gas!"

Chapter

Twelve

WHAT ARE YOU TALKING ABOUT?" Adam demanded.

"Gas," Nancy explained. "I noticed it a few moments ago, but I couldn't place the smell."

"I smell it, too," Bess put in. "That's what I've been trying to tell you."

Paula gave Bess a dismissive look. "Big deal. I'll get the plumber to come in this afternoon."

Nancy shook her head decisively. "It's a little late for that. The smell is getting stronger. If I'm not mistaken, one stray spark and this place could blow up."

"I'm sure you're overreacting," Paula said.

"Perhaps," Nancy said. "But I'm not taking chances with the lives of your staff and customers. Now, why don't we finish this conversation outside?"

Nancy raised her eyebrows at George and Bess, sending them a silent signal that said, "I want you out now!"

"I'll go tell the kitchen staff," George said calmly. She carefully let herself out of the office.

"I'll tell the wait staff and anyone else who's in the dining room," Bess said, and followed George.

"Are we really going to do this?" Paula demanded of Adam. "Close the restaurant again? The papers will love it!"

Adam ran his fingers through his long hair and looked from Paula's face to Nancy's. "I trust Nancy's opinion," Adam finally said. "I want you to help George and Bess get everyone outside."

"Adam—" Paula started to argue.

"Go!" Adam said shortly.

Paula turned and stormed out of the office.

"After you," Adam said to Nancy as he got to his feet.

"I'm not leaving just yet," Nancy said.

"What? Why not?" Adam demanded.

"Someone has to go down to the basement and shut off the gas," Nancy told him.

"Good idea," Adam said. "I'll go with you."

"No," Nancy said.

"Listen, I'm not negotiating with you," Adam told her. "Move!"

They stepped into the kitchen together. The outside door was open, and Nancy saw George urging the staff to leave immediately.

"Who'd have thought a restaurant was such a dangerous place to work?" Mitch was loudly saying to Meghan as they made their way to the door.

Meghan caught Nancy's eye. Nancy noticed that Meghan was wiping her hands nervously on her chef's coat. Nancy did her best to give Meghan a reassuring smile. Working in Reverb's kitchen was practically like working in a combat zone. She led Adam toward the basement stairs and started down.

But Adam paused at the top of the flight. "I can't see where I'm going," he complained. "Aren't you going to turn on the light?"

"No," Nancy said. "Electrical circuits can cause sparks. It's safer this way. Come down a few steps and then stop for a second and let your eyes adjust."

"Fine," Adam grumbled. He stopped on the step above Nancy.

Nancy was twitching with an overwhelming desire to get out of the building. But she stood still until her eyes adjusted to the darkness. "Okay," Nancy whispered. "Let's go."

Nancy led the way down the creaky steps. Two small, dirt-spattered windows near the basement's ceiling let in just enough light for Nancy to see a mess of wires and pipes tangled up against the wall. But she could not make out which one was the gas line.

There was a loud noise behind her, followed by a shout from Adam. Nancy instantly turned.

"Argh!" Adam exclaimed. "Who left this tool box sitting in the middle of the floor?"

"Shh! Do you hear that?" Nancy asked.

Adam leaned over to rub his shin. "Hear what?"

"Hissing," Nancy said. "It's coming from over there!"

"With my luck lately it's probably a couple of hungry rattlesnakes," Adam said.

"No snakes," Nancy said as she carefully made her way to a panel on the wall. She could just make out a slender pipe that had a red knob on it. "It's the gas line," she whispered.

"Can you turn it off?" Adam asked.

"I'm trying," Nancy said as she carefully turned the knob several rotations clockwise. The intensity of the hissing didn't change. "Okay, then it's got to be the other way," Nancy whispered. She twisted the knob counterclockwise. One turn. Two. Three. The hissing continued.

"What's happening?" Adam demanded.

Nancy stepped closer to the slender pipe and carefully examined it in the half-light. "Someone has deliberately put a hole in the pipe!" she exclaimed.

"Can we stop it up somehow?" Adam asked.

"No," Nancy quickly decided. "Let's just get out of here."

"I thought you were never going to say that," Adam said. "Let's go!"

Nancy led the way across the basement and back up the steps. She had to keep herself from panicking, from running. *I hope Bess or George* called the fire department, Nancy was thinking as she reached the top of the stairs. She glanced back to make sure Adam was still right behind her.

As Nancy and Adam hurried across the kitchen, Nancy saw a blur of movement through one of the back windows, which, she noted absently, was open. For a split second, she almost caught sight of a face, but it was gone before she could see it clearly. At exactly the same moment that the face disappeared, Nancy heard a familiar sound—a match being struck.

A match!

We have to get outside, Nancy thought. "Run!" she yelled to Adam.

But she was too late. An enormous blast threw Nancy off her feet. In a series of quick, confused flashes, Nancy saw the kitchen floor seeming to rise up to meet her.

She hit the floor hard. The impact set her sliding across the room on her back. Nancy had just enough time to cover her head with her arms before she crashed into the bottom of a stainless steel counter.

Adam, Nancy thought. She wanted to call to him, to make sure he was all right. But before she could, everything went black.

Chapter

Thirteen

N<small>AN</small>? N<small>AN</small>, can you hear me?"

Nancy struggled back to consciousness. Gradually she realized that someone was bending over her, urging her to wake up. It was a familiar voice. Bess.

"Please, Nan," the voice said gently.

Nancy drew in her breath. With an immense effort, she forced her eyes open. As her vision cleared, she saw Bess standing over her. But there was someone else, too. A man she didn't recognize. Slowly, painfully Nancy sat up far enough to discover that she was lying on a narrow cot with a green blanket pulled over her.

The strange man leaned forward and firmly pushed Nancy's shoulders back into the cot. "Take it easy, now," he said.

"What—" Nancy started. But then the memory of the explosion came rushing back to her. She turned her head slightly and saw a cluster of medical instruments just inches from her nose. An ambulance, Nancy thought groggily. But it wasn't moving.

And then suddenly a more urgent thought caused her to sit upright. "Where's Adam?" Nancy asked. She had sat up so quickly that the scene before her faded into blackness for an instant. When her vision returned, it was accompanied by a persistent throbbing in her head.

"Whoa!" the stranger said. "Lie back and rest. You have a nasty bump on the head."

Nancy explored her head with her fingers and found an enormous bump just behind her right ear. She touched it ever so slightly and winced in pain. "Do I have a concussion?" Nancy asked.

"Well, let's have a look," the paramedic said.

"Does that mean I can sit up?" Nancy asked.

The paramedic nodded, and Bess rushed forward to help. Nancy sat up slowly and let the paramedic shine a tiny flashlight into her eyes.

"Do you know your name?" the paramedic asked.

"Yes, it's Nancy Drew," Nancy told him.

"Can you spell it?" the paramedic asked.

Nancy smiled at Bess. But Bess was all business, frowning in concern. Nancy sighed and obediently spelled her name.

"You don't seem to have a concussion," the paramedic started to say, "but—"

"Great," Nancy interrupted, and shook off the blanket.

"Where are you going?" the paramedic demanded. "You have to go to the hospital and let the doctors check you out. You've suffered a serious blow."

"Not the first," Nancy told him. She knew that if her injuries were really serious, the ambulance would have been on its way to the hospital immediately. "I promise to see a doctor soon. But right now I have more important things to worry about."

"Then you'll have to sign a release form," the paramedic said.

"Fine," Nancy said. "Give it to me." She quickly signed the form.

"Are you sure you're okay?" Bess asked as she helped Nancy down from the ambulance.

Nancy nodded as she took in the scene outside Reverb. It was a replay of the opening night. Employees were standing around in groups, waiting and gossiping. Ambulances had been pulled up at angles to the curb. The place was already crawling with police, and Nancy knew it wouldn't be long before the reporters started to arrive.

"I could use an aspirin," Nancy admitted, giving her friend a reassuring wink. "But I think I'll live. Where's Adam?"

"They hid him away in another ambulance," Bess said in a low tone.

Nancy's eyes widened in alarm. "Is he okay?"

126

Bess giggled. "Yes, fine. He's sort of using the ambulance as a temporary office."

"How did he talk the paramedics into that?" Nancy asked. "They're going to lose their jobs if anyone finds out."

"They're big Void fans," she explained. "Anyway, don't worry about Adam. George is with him. She thought someone should stay with him."

"Good plan," Nancy said. "I'm pretty sure now that someone wants him—" She trailed off as she caught sight of Reverb. The explosion had knocked the glass out of the windows, and the firefighters had hacked the front door off its hinges. The late-afternoon sunlight was spilling in through the door, and Nancy could see that the floor was covered with rubble.

Bess followed Nancy's gaze and shook her head sadly. "The restaurant's a total mess. Adam's going to have to spend a lot of time and money before he can open again."

"If he decides to open again," Nancy said.

"He will," Bess said. "I don't think Adam would like anyone calling him a quitter. Especially someone like Larry."

"You're right!" Nancy laughed as she and Bess made their way to the other ambulance. They found George standing outside, her arms crossed and a sour look on her face. But George smiled when she saw Nancy. "Hey, are you okay? I was worried about you!"

127

"I'm fine," Nancy said. "But what are you doing out here?"

George groaned. "Adam kicked me out while he got a damage report."

Nancy's eyes narrowed. "Who's in there with him?"

"Paula," George said.

"Where's the paramedic?" Nancy asked, suddenly growing alarmed.

"Probably off flirting with one of the waitresses," George said. "Adam's not seriously hurt—" George stopped when she saw the look on Nancy's face. "You don't think—"

"Paula is one of our prime suspects." Nancy stepped forward and rapped on the door of the ambulance.

Relief flooded over Nancy when Adam himself immediately swung the door outward. He jumped out of the ambulance, but winced and stumbled as his feet hit the ground.

"Adam, I really don't think you should be walking around," Paula yelled after him.

Adam turned and pointed a finger at her. "I'm not that interested in your advice," he said. Paula's face drained of color as Adam continued. "I want to see how bad the damage is. And then I want to see that the creep who did this spends a good long time behind bars!"

Adam started across the parking lot toward the restaurant. In spite of a pronounced limp, he was moving quickly. Nancy, Bess, and George hurried after him. They were still crossing the parking lot when Frank drove up in his little white hatchback. Adam noticed the car, too. He stopped walking and waited while Frank pulled into a parking space.

As Frank climbed out of the car, he surveyed the scene around him, looking dazed. He caught George's eye and smiled, but he immediately turned to his boss. "Adam, what's going on? I saw the ambulances and the police—"

"I know that!" Adam snapped. "What I want to know now is where have you been."

"Um—" Frank paused as if unsure of how to best answer. "I've been food shopping. You know that's what I do every morning."

"Yeah, sure, and it's almost eleven." Adam sneered.

Frank exploded. "Listen, I've had enough of your paranoid suspicions. If you don't believe me, take a look!" He walked around the car and popped the back open. Inside were boxes overflowing with fresh fruits and vegetables.

"So?" Adam shot back. "How do I know when you bought that?"

Frank took a step toward Adam. "You could try going to the farmers' market and asking," he suggested. "I stopped by at least a dozen stands there this morning."

Some of the Reverb employees who were standing nearby turned their heads toward the group when they heard Adam and Frank's harsh exchange. Nancy caught Meghan's eye. She was surprised by the pastry chef's almost vacant

129

expression. But for the moment, Nancy had some more immediate concerns.

Adam clenched his fists in anger and stepped even closer to Frank. "Don't tell me what to do," he said right into Frank's face. "I'm the boss around here. You're just one of my many employees."

"Come on, you guys." Nancy stepped between the two of them. "Calm down. This isn't helping."

"Get out of my way." Adam turned his eyes away from Frank just long enough to shoot Nancy an angry look. "I told you that I fight my own fights!"

Frank had been waiting for an opening. Before anyone could stop him, he stepped forward and hit Adam with a well-timed punch square to the jaw.

The force of the punch made Adam take a step backward. For a split second, he looked stunned. But he quickly raised his fists. "You want to fight, huh? Then come on, let's fight!"

Chapter

Fourteen

EVEN NANCY was momentarily frozen in place as Frank and Adam engaged in a fierce struggle. Then she had an idea. She rushed over to Frank's car and reached into a box of beefsteak tomatoes and grabbed two. She expertly aimed the tomatoes in rapid succession at the brawling men. She hit Adam squarely on the forehead and Frank on the side of his neck.

Both men stopped in their tracks. They were dusty, sweaty, and dripping with tomato juice. Frank stared at her openmouthed. Adam immediately began to yell, but Nancy abruptly cut him off.

"I'm sorry, guys, but I had to do it," she said firmly. "Listen, you may not have noticed, but that bombed-out shell of a restaurant would suggest that we've got a serious situation here.

And fighting isn't going to help us solve it. Now, let's go inside."

Adam and Frank silently followed Nancy into the restaurant, where she led them to a table in the corner, carefully stepping over the debris. George, Bess, and Paula followed a few steps behind.

Adam glared at Frank angrily. "You have some explaining to do, my friend."

"He's right, Frank," Nancy agreed. "Where have you been all morning?"

"I told you, I was shopping. On my way back to the restaurant, there was a major traffic jam— a tractor-trailer overturned—and I was stuck for an hour. I'm sure you can check that out, and talk to my guys at the farmers' market." Frank looked at Adam. "Come on, man. You know I'd never do something stupid like this." He gestured to the wreck all around them.

"Maybe not," Adam answered, "but I need to know who did, and I need to know *now.*"

"All right," Nancy said. "Let's talk this through. First, who had access to the keys to the freezer and when?" She took a deep breath and looked down for a moment. Suddenly something caught her eye. She found herself looking again at Paula's loafers.

"Paula, I have to ask you something. What are all those tiny spots on your shoes?"

Paula looked down. "How should I know?" she answered defiantly.

"Let me help. It's cake batter," Nancy told her.

"That mixer in the kitchen throws batter everywhere, especially on anyone who stands too close. Like Meghan, for instance. I noticed she was wearing shoes exactly like those yesterday. She probably didn't bother to clean them before returning them to her roommate."

"The roommate Paula was so anxious to hide!" George said.

"What does that prove?" Paula said. "So she's my roommate. I haven't done anything wrong, and neither has she. Any other big evidence you'd like to share?"

At this moment a sad, soft voice spoke up. "Never mind, Paula. You don't have to stick up for me. I can take care of this unfinished business with Adam all by myself."

Nancy caught her breath as she turned to see Meghan calmly walk up behind where Adam was sitting and point an enormous chef's knife an inch from his throat. Paula screamed.

"Everyone please step back," Meghan said evenly.

Adam's eyes were open unnaturally wide. His nostrils flared as he took deep, shaky breaths through his nose. He was holding his body rigid, fighting not to move.

But Meghan's hands were shaking so hard that the knife lightly grazed Adam's neck. A bead of bright red blood appeared on Adam's skin.

"Get back," she repeated. "Or I'll kill him. I mean it."

Nancy didn't doubt it for a moment. Nancy

nodded at the others, indicating that they should retreat.

But Paula gingerly inched forward. "Come on, Meghan," she said as if she were speaking to a frightened child. "You don't really want to hurt Adam. Wouldn't you be lonely without him?"

Meghan shook her head wildly. "Nope. I wouldn't miss him at all. He deserves to die."

Paula laughed nervously. "Maybe he does. But let's be selfish for a minute. Without Adam, there wouldn't be any more new Void albums. And that would definitely be a bummer."

Meghan gazed down at Adam for just a second, as if considering that thought. Nancy saw her opening. In a flash, she dashed behind Meghan, hitting her right elbow with the side of her open hand as hard as possible.

The blow caused Meghan reflexively to open her hand. The knife clattered to the ground.

Meghan made a lunge for the knife, but Nancy was faster. She quickly kicked the knife out of Meghan's reach. For a moment, Meghan remained motionless on her hands and knees, staring at the knife with longing. Then she sprang to her feet and shoved Nancy as hard as she could. As Nancy fell, Meghan ran toward the kitchen door at top speed.

"Get her!" Nancy yelled.

George took off in a flash after Meghan. Nancy scrambled to her feet and followed. The two girls tackled Meghan in the parking lot. By the time

they got her to her feet, Adam, Frank, and Paula
had reached them, as had a police officer.

"I'll take over now," the officer said. He hand-
cuffed Meghan, who offered no resistance.

"Does someone want to explain what's going
on here?" the officer asked.

"Sure. I will," Adam offered. "That girl you've
got in cuffs tried to electrocute me, caused the
explosion in my restaurant, and just tried to kill
me with a knife about this long," he said, gesturing a twelve-inch span with his hands.

The officer looked at Meghan. She was silent.

"Well, I'm going to need all of you to come
down to the station and give us statements."

"We'll be there," Nancy promised.

As they walked toward their cars, Nancy made
her way over to Adam. "Are you okay?"

He reached up and gently touched his throat.
"Yes, thanks to you and Paula. But for a while
there, I thought I'd sung my last song."

Adam walked over to Paula, who was sobbing
quietly. "Hey, Paula, don't take it so hard," he
said. "You can get a new roommate. Or better
yet, I'll give you a raise so you won't need one."

Paula spun toward Adam and beat her fists
against his chest. "You idiot. Meghan's not just
my roommate. She's my sister. My baby sister.
And you've ruined her life!"

135

Chapter

Fifteen

H EY, FOLKS, I bet you thought we forgot about you!" A paunchy policeman named Officer Brooks walked into the dingy room at the station where Nancy and Adam had been sitting at a table for hours. Bess and George had finished giving their statements sometime earlier, so they'd headed back to the hotel. But Nancy and Adam had given their statements and then were asked to remain.

"Not at all," Nancy said politely.

"Speak for yourself!" Adam exploded. "What's going on here? I've been here so long I'm beginning to feel like the suspect."

Officer Brooks rubbed his eyes under his glasses and shook his head. "We were interrogating Ms. Moore. She gave us a full confession."

"Great!" Nancy said.

"That's not all." Officer Brooks crossed the room and poured himself a cup of coffee. "She gave us the name of a ministorage place off the highway. A couple of uniforms went out there and it checked out." He winked at Adam. "They're bringing your property in even as we speak."

Adam's mood changed immediately. He slapped his hand against the table. "Yes!"

"Congratulations!" Nancy smiled at Adam and then turned her attention back to Officer Brooks. "What has Meghan been charged with?"

"Sabotage, arson, grand larceny—that's for the guitars—and the big one: attempted murder," Officer Brooks reeled off. "If a jury finds her guilty, she should be put away for a long time."

"Good," Adam said bitterly.

Officer Brooks studied him curiously. "That little lady really hates you. What did you do to her anyway?"

"I didn't do anything to her!" Adam burst out. "I hardly even knew her. The chick is a nut!" Adam let out a heavy sigh. "Sometimes I wish I'd become a plumber or something."

Officer Brooks looked down at Adam's thousand-dollar cowboy boots and raised his eyebrows. "Sure. Whatever you say."

"Can we go now?" Nancy asked.

"Yes," Officer Brooks said. "Now that Ms. Moore has confessed, we won't need additional

137

information—at least not for now. Thanks for your cooperation."

Adam grabbed his leather jacket and followed Nancy. "I can't wait to get out of here," he muttered as they made their way down the hallway. "I'm exhausted."

"The past few days have been pretty intense," Nancy agreed.

"And now I've got to go back to Reverb and make sure everything there is secured," Adam said.

"Adam, look who's here," she added as they turned a corner in the hallway. Nancy had just spotted Paula sitting on a wooden bench against one wall.

Paula had seen them, too. She stood up and waited for them to approach her.

"What should I do?" Adam whispered to Nancy.

"Let's hear what she has to say," Nancy said.

"Hi," Paula said in a husky voice, giving them a shaky smile. The strain of the day's events showed on her face. Her skin looked sallow, and dark circles had appeared under her eyes. Nancy's heart went out to her.

"Are you okay, Paula?" Nancy asked.

"Yeah, fine," Paula said with a little shiver. She fixed her eyes on Adam. "I'd like a chance to explain what happened," she told him.

"Go ahead," Adam said.

"Not here," Paula told him. "Could we go somewhere?"

Adam shifted his weight and sighed. "I need to get back to the restaurant. I have a big mess to deal with there."

"Please, Adam," Paula said, blinking back tears.

Nancy put a hand on Adam's arm. "Would you feel better if I came?" she whispered to him.

"Definitely," Adam said. "I don't want to be alone with the psycho's sister."

Nancy glanced at her watch. She'd promised to have dinner with Bess and George, and she only had ten minutes to get to the restaurant where they'd agreed to meet. "I don't have much time today, and we've all been through a lot. Why don't we meet tomorrow morning in the coffee shop at my hotel? By then we may all feel a little calmer."

"Fine," Adam said shortly.

"Thank you," Paula told Nancy sincerely.

Nancy was twenty minutes late to meet her friends. She rushed into the restaurant where they'd agreed to meet just in time to see a waiter place a steaming deep-dish pizza in front of Bess, George, and Frank.

"Good timing," George greeted her.

"Sorry I'm late," Nancy said. She turned to Frank. "I didn't know you were meeting us, but I'm glad you could."

"Yeah, we're really glad you weren't busy elsewhere," Bess said in a meaningful tone.

George and Nancy smiled.

"What's so funny?" Frank demanded.

Nancy shrugged. "For a little while we had a theory that you might have been behind the sabotage at Reverb."

Frank's mouth dropped open. "You suspected me, too? Not just Adam?"

Nancy nodded.

"George didn't think so," Bess commented.

"You stood up for me?" Frank asked George. George nodded.

"Thanks," Frank said. "That means a lot to me." He leaned over and gave her a quick kiss on the cheek. Then he seemed to reconsider, and he kissed her gently on the lips.

Bess looked away and smiled, raising her glass of soda in a toast. "Here's to another case solved."

Nancy clicked Bess's glass with her own. "Here's to friends," she added, looking around the table and smiling.

The next morning Nancy was the first one packed. She couldn't wait to climb into the Mustang and head for home. She wasn't looking forward to meeting Paula and Adam for coffee. When it came time for Nancy to go downstairs, George was still packing and Bess had just gotten out of the shower.

"Do you want me to settle up with the hotel while I'm downstairs?" Nancy asked her friends.

"No way," George said. "We can't check out yet. Frank is coming over to say goodbye."

"Again?" Nancy teased her. "What do you call last night?"

George gave her a wink. "A warm-up."

"Well, I hope the main event doesn't take too long," Nancy joked. "I wanted to get home sometime today."

George laughed. "I promise you it will be a very fast goodbye. With Reverb closed for who knows how long, Frank is looking for a new job. I told him that if he can't find anything in Chicago, River Heights can use another good chef."

"Well, I don't want to get in the way of true love, so I'll get out of here as soon as Frank arrives," Bess said. "I'll check us out and finish packing the car. We can pick you up in front of the coffee shop, Nan."

"Great," Nancy said, tossing Bess her car keys. "See you in about an hour."

Nancy went down to the little coffee shop and slid into a booth. A few minutes later, Paula and Adam arrived at almost exactly the same time. Adam had his long, shiny hair pulled back into a ponytail and a baseball cap pulled down over his eyes. Nancy guessed he was hoping nobody would recognize him.

But nobody was paying attention as Adam and Paula joined Nancy in the booth. The waitress brought them coffee. After she was gone, Adam gave Paula a challenging look. "Okay, I'm here," he said. "What do you want?"

Paula looked better than she had the night

before, Nancy thought. She'd chosen her clothes with care, and her makeup had been perfectly applied. But her eyes were drooping, and Nancy guessed she hadn't slept much.

Before answering Adam, Paula set her coffee cup down and took a deep breath. "I want to ask you to drop the charges against Meghan."

"And what makes you think I'd do that, even if I could?" Adam asked harshly.

Paula met Adam's angry gaze with a defiant look. "Because Meghan only did this out of love for you."

"Love?" Adam snorted. "Is that supposed to be funny?"

"No, it's true," Paula insisted. "My sister has been your biggest fan since she was twelve years old. As soon as she got her driver's license she started following Void across the country. She wrote you hundreds of letters, Adam."

"So do lots of girls," Adam said with an edge of arrogance.

"I realize that," Paula said evenly. "Anyway, when Meghan was about seventeen she managed to get front-row tickets to one of your concerts. You sang a love song. I can't remember the name of it, but Meghan would know. You came down off the stage and sang directly to Meghan."

"I know what song it was," Adam said. "I sang it to some girl in the front row during every concert that tour."

Paula gave Adam an impatient look. "I'm sure that picking Meghan out of the crowd wasn't a

142

big deal to you. But it convinced her that the two of you had some deep connection."

"That should have been enough to tell you she needed help," Adam said.

"It was," Paula said. "I tried to tell her it wasn't a big deal. But she wouldn't listen. I told my mom and stepfather—Meghan's father—that Meghan needed counseling. But they thought I was overreacting.

"Their solution was to forbid Meghan to go to any more Void concerts. She was miserable. And she was worried about you, Adam. She had this nutty idea that you wouldn't be able to perform without her being there. When Void came to our hometown, Meghan sent you a telegram. She explained she couldn't come to the concert, and she begged you to come to our house to see her."

"I get hundreds of invitations like that when I'm on tour," Adam said impatiently. "Are you suggesting I go to every crackpot's house?"

"I'm not suggesting anything," Paula said. "I'm just telling you what happened!"

"Fine," Adam said tightly. "Go on."

"When Adam didn't show up, Meghan was heartbroken," Paula told Nancy. "It was as if she suddenly realized he didn't know she was alive. She was so furious, she destroyed all of her Void CDs and burned the scrapbooks she had spent years putting together. But then she seemed to get over it."

"How did Meghan react when she heard you were working for Adam?" Nancy asked.

Paula stared down at her coffee cup for a long moment. "She had just graduated from cooking school," Paula finally said. "As I remember, she hardly asked me about Adam. She seemed more interested in the restaurant and the menu we were planning."

"Did she ask you to get her a job?" Nancy said.

Paula nodded. "She was having a hard time finding a job in Louisville—that's where we're from. I'd only been in Chicago about a year, and I thought it would be fun to have my baby sister around. Even though we're half-sisters, we've always been close. But I made her a promise to keep the fact that we were sisters secret."

"Why?" Adam asked.

"Would you have let me hire her if you knew she was my sister?" Paula asked.

"Probably not," Adam admitted.

"Meghan really is a sweet kid." Paula swallowed hard and shook her head. "I'm sorry for all the trouble she caused." Paula ran her finger around the lip of her cup. "The truth is I suspected her. But I guess I just couldn't imagine her doing something so awful. I thought everything would be okay if I just kept an eye on her."

"Listen, it's not your fault," Adam told Paula. "She needs professional help. She probably needs the kind of help she won't get in prison."

"So you'll drop the charges?" Paula asked.

"Paula," Adam said quietly, "it's too late. It's out of my hands. Arson, sabotage, attempted murder, grand larceny? It's not up to me. But what I will do is ask for leniency, and I'll do everything I can to make sure she gets all the help she needs."

"That's great, Adam," Nancy said, a bit surprised by his generosity and understanding.

Paula reached across the table and squeezed Adam's hand. "Thanks. I can't ask for more than that."

"You don't need to thank me, Paula," Adam said. "Actually I'm looking out for myself. Last night, when I got back to Reverb, there were hundreds of decisions to make. I didn't know what to do. Paula, I need your help if I'm ever going to reopen."

Paula and Nancy stared at Adam in disbelief for a moment. Then Paula smiled broadly. Nancy realized it was the first time she'd ever seen Paula smile.

"Thanks for the offer, Adam," Paula said, shaking her head with a smile. "But I can't go back to Reverb. After everything that's happened, it would just be too hard."

Adam groaned. "If you don't come back, I'm going to sell the dump to Whitney."

Paula laughed. "Come on, Adam. Don't give up so easily. I'm sure that if you look, you'll find a daily manager who's even meaner than I am."

"Impossible," Adam told her, and grinned.

"Listen, I have to go," Paula said, getting to her feet. "I have a slew of lawyers to talk to."

"Okay," Adam told Paula. He stood up to give her a hug, apparently sincerely sad to see her go. Nancy could tell Adam admired his hard-as-nails manager.

Nancy admired Paula, too, but for a different reason. Most people would have abandoned Meghan after all the trouble she had caused. "Good luck," Nancy called as Paula headed for the door.

Paula waved on her way out.

"I have a business proposition for you, too," Adam told Nancy when they were alone.

"Really?" Nancy asked.

"Really," Adam said. "This whole thing with Meghan has made me realize how many crazed fans I have. So, how'd you like to stick around and be my personal bodyguard?"

"Bodyguard?" Nancy repeated. "I've done it on a temporary basis before, but that's not my usual thing."

"Don't say no until you hear about the fringe benefits," Adam told her.

"Fringe benefits?" Nancy joked. "You mean like a free checkup at the dentist once a year?"

"No," Adam told her. "I mean a chance for us to get to know each other better. Void's going on a major tour next month. We could see some of the most romantic places in the world together."

A series of images flashed through Nancy's head. She saw herself at Adam's side in Rome. And lying next to him on a beautiful beach on the French Riviera. She saw herself standing backstage at concerts, alert for trouble. Nancy Drew, bodyguard to the rich and famous . . . Yuck, she thought.

Nancy shook her head. "Sorry, Adam. It sounds like fun, but I'm really happy doing what I do now. And after the weekend you showed me here in Chicago, I'll be happy to stay put in River Heights for a while."

"I can't believe this," Adam said. "Two rejections in five minutes. It totally blows my average."

Nancy was laughing when she heard the sound of a familiar beep. She looked out the coffee shop's window and saw her blue Mustang idling at the curb. "I have to go," she told Adam.

"But what about us?" Adam asked, with a sad face as Nancy stood.

From what Nancy knew about Adam, she couldn't believe their little flirtation was going to change his life. She leaned over and gave him a quick kiss on the forehead.

"If you're not over me in twenty-four hours, write a song about it," Nancy told Adam, then grinned. " 'Bye now."

Adam returned her grin. " 'Bye," he said. "Listen for that song!"

Nancy headed for the door. Before walking outside she turned to wave at Adam. She saw that a beautiful girl with long red hair had approached his booth. She was smiling at Adam stupidly. He gestured for her to sit down. Adam doesn't need me, Nancy told herself, and smiled. He has his fans.

When George saw Nancy hurrying toward the Mustang, she got out of the driver's seat so that Nancy could get in.

Nancy noted her friend's happy look. "Did you have a good long goodbye with Frank?" she teased George.

"I didn't say goodbye," George told her. "He's coming to River Heights next weekend."

"That's great," Nancy said. "Now that we know that he's not a criminal, I think he's a pretty great guy."

"Very funny!" George said as she crawled into the backseat.

Nancy got into the car, put on her seat belt, and pulled out into traffic. "So, did everything go okay at the hotel?" she asked.

"Fine," Bess said. "Oh, and Ned called. He said he's coming home from school for the weekend and he'll stop by your house this evening. And he told me to tell you he can't wait to see you."

Nancy grinned and hit the gas. "That's the best news I've heard all day!"

Nancy's next case:

Nancy's old friend Angela Chamberlain is getting married, and Nancy's come to her family's opulent Long Island estate to be a bridesmaid. But love and money can be a very volatile mix. It becomes clear, before the ink is dry on the invitations, that the date is set for danger and that Nancy will have to stand up for Angela in more ways than one. The romance between Angela and her fiancé has suddenly taken an ugly turn. Sinister rumors, hints of scandal, and whispers of betrayal have begun to surface. With them come a series of near fatal "accidents," culminating in attempted murder. If Nancy doesn't uncover the culprit soon, Angela's dream wedding could end in nightmare . . . in *Betrayed by Love,* Case #118 in The Nancy Drew Files™.

Christopher Pike presents....
a frighteningly fun new series for your younger brothers and sisters!

1	The Secret Path	53725-3/$3.50
2	The Howling Ghost	53726-1/$3.50
3	The Haunted Cave	53727-X/$3.50
4	Aliens in the Sky	53728-8/$3.99
5	The Cold People	55064-0/$3.99
6	The Witch's Revenge	55065-9/$3.99
7	The Dark Corner	55066-7/$3.99
8	The Little People	55067-5/$3.99
9	The Wishing Stone	55068-3/$3.99
10	The Wicked Cat	55069-1/$3.99
11	The Deadly Past	55072-1/$3.99
12	The Hidden Beast	55073-X/$3.99
13	The Creature in the Teacher	00261-9/$3.99
14	The Evil House	00262-7/$3.99
15	Invasion of the No-Ones	00263-5/$3.99
16	Time Terror	00264-3/$3.99

A MINSTREL® BOOK

R·L·STINE'S
GHOSTS OF FEAR STREET®

Nancy Drew on Campus™

By Carolyn Keene

- ☐ 1 New Lives, New Loves — 52737-1/$3.99
- ☐ 2 On Her Own — 52741-X/$3.99
- ☐ 3 Don't Look Back — 52744-4/$3.99
- ☐ 4 Tell Me The Truth — 52745-2/$3.99
- ☐ 5 Secret Rules — 52746-0/$3.99
- ☐ 6 It's Your Move — 52748-7/$3.99
- ☐ 7 False Friends — 52751-7/$3.99
- ☐ 8 Getting Closer — 52754-1/$3.99
- ☐ 9 Broken Promises — 52757-6/$3.99
- ☐ 10 Party Weekend — 52758-4/$3.99
- ☐ 11 In the Name of Love — 52759-2/$3.99
- ☐ 12 Just the Two of Us — 52764-9/$3.99
- ☐ 13 Campus Exposures — 56802-7/$3.99
- ☐ 14 Hard to Get — 56803-5/$3.99
- ☐ 15 Loving and Losing — 56804-3/$3.99
- ☐ 16 Going Home — 56805-1/$3.99
- ☐ 17 New Beginnings — 56806-X/$3.99
- ☐ 18 Keeping Secrets — 56807-8/$3.99
- ☐ 19 Love On-Line — 00211-2/$3.99
- ☐ 20 Jealous Feelings — 00212-0/$3.99

Available from Archway Paperbacks